The New Atlantis
and Other Early
Science Fiction Tales

www.firestonebooks.com

The New Atlantis
and Other Early Science Fiction Tales

2013 Edition
Published by Firestone Books

Translation copyright © Firestone Books
Edited by David Lear

ISBN: 978-1-909608-07-8

Printed and bound by CreateSpace, USA

www.firestonebooks.com

You can also find out more by following Firestone
Books on Facebook and Twitter

Contents

Introduction

Many people could be forgiven for thinking that concepts such as voyages into space, time travel, robots and extraterrestrials started in the nineteenth century with the works of Jules Verne, HG Wells and other science fiction pioneers. In truth, however, these ideas have far earlier origins, dating back a thousand years and more.

The beginnings of science fiction are hard, if not impossible to date. The Indian epic tale *Ramayana*, for instance, written around 500BC, tells of flying vehicles that could travel into space, but the story as a whole is fantasy with only a grain of science fiction. Going to the other extreme, it could be said that science fiction didn't begin until the mid-nineteenth century with the works of Jules Verne, whose tales were often founded on up-to-date science and futuristic technology.

For this collection of science fiction we have decided to cast the net widely and include stories which, while they may not be purely of this genre, are of historical interest and do contain at least some science fiction. For the purpose of this first volume we have started with Cicero's *Dream of Scipio*, written around 51BC, and our collection ends with Francis Bacon's *The New Atlantis*, first published in 1624.

There is a break in European science fiction of around fifteen hundred years, from the decline of the

Greek and Roman cultures, until the beginning of the seventeenth century. This hibernation and subsequent reawakening had a number of causes:

During the dark ages there was a scarcity of written works in general. In medieval times the idea of life on other planets was viewed by many as heresy, so it is quite likely that writers judiciously avoided such subject matter.

In terms of the rebirth of science fiction, there were numerous factors, such as the declining power of the Church, and the advent of the printing press. There was also the circumnavigation of the Earth, meaning the world, which once must have seemed to have endless oceans and unlimited possibilities, now appeared to be a smaller and less interesting place. This meant fantasy writers had to look beneath the waves, underground, and out into space, for backdrops to their exotic tales.

The greatest influence on the pioneers of this genre however, was the rise of modern science, where the mysteries of life and the universe, were explained by observation and reason, rather than by supernatural belief. Writers who wished to create believable fantasy could no longer employ magic in their tales, and instead turned to speculative technology – the basis of much science fiction to this day.

The Dream of Scipio

Cicero

Introduction

Marcus Tullius Cicero (106BC–43BC) was a Roman philosopher, statesman and lawyer who, after a power struggle with Mark Anthony, was declared an enemy of the state and consequently murdered in 43BC.

The Dream of Scipio was written in 51BC, and is a fictional tale of General Scipio Aemilianus, a real person who lived 185BC–129BC. In the tale, Scipio's dream takes him into space where he meets his dead ancestors, and where he also views the Moon, Sun, stars and planets. He also sees how insignificant the Earth, the Roman Empire and human life are when compared with the majesty of the Universe. As to whether or not Scipio's soul actually ascended into space, or if it was simply a dream, is never revealed.

The Dream of Scipio

Cicero

When I was posted to Africa to serve as military tribune to the Fourth Legion, under General Manilius, I thought I might use the opportunity to pay a visit to King Masinissa, who had been a friend of the family for many years.

I travelled to his home and was escorted to his room where the old king embraced me and, to my surprise, began to cry.

"Praise be to the Sun and the Heavens," he wept. "Young Scipio has managed to pay me a visit before I depart from this life. Scipio – the mere mentioning of your name makes me feel young again. Looking at you now I can see so much of your grandfather, Africanus, in you. I don't need to tell you what a brilliant and fearless man he was, I'm sure."

After his kind words, we sat down and talked both of my Republic and his Kingdom. We had much to say, and the conversation was so interesting that the evening seemed to come all too quickly.

We ate and were soon after treated to the most spectacular entertainment, but instead of retiring to bed afterwards we continued our conversation. King Masinissa told me tales of my grandfather's exploits that I had never heard until now, and he imparted many wise words that my grandfather had, long ago, told him.

Eventually, the desire for sleep began to overwhelm us both and we were compelled to make our separate ways to bed. I shared a room with Laelius and others who were already slumbering, and after my long journey, and having stayed up so late, I quickly fell to sleep.

I have no doubt that all that we see and hear during the day, and preceding days, influence our dreams, and this night I soon found myself floating among the stars, and staring at someone familiar, but whose identity I could not fathom at first.

At last, as my earliest memories were trawled and I recalled a painting I had seen in my childhood, I realized I was face-to-face with my grandfather, Africanus. My blood chilled and I could not help but shudder.

"Do not be afraid, Scipio," my grandfather reassured. "I am here to help you, so listen carefully to all I say, and make sure you remember all I have said when you wake."

We were floating far above the Earth, and my grandfather pointed.

"You see that city?"

"Carthage?" I asked.

"Yes," he replied. "Long ago I used an army to conquer that town, and I made sure that they submitted to the will of the Roman people, but over time the citizens there have started to become restless. You in your capacity as a private soldier will soon be sent there to attack Carthage, and within two years you, as

Consul, will destroy that city. After that you will be made Censor, and you will embark on missions across Egypt, Syria, Asia Minor and Greece. During your your absence from the Roman Republic, your homeland, you will be elected as Consul a second time. With your growing power, you will bring an end to a most important war, and you will raze Numantia to the ground."

I was pleased to hear that my future sounded so fabulous, but before I could tell my grandfather, he warned me.

"You must at all times be aware of my other grandson, Tiberius. He is a schemer, and you would do well to keep your eye on him. When you eventually return to the Capitol, you will find the Republic greatly troubled by his evil ways. It is for you to save the Republic from him, and to do this, you must use all your courage and intelligence. As to whether or not you will be successful, I cannot say. After this point the future becomes shrouded in fog, through which I cannot see.

"At this time all the people of the Republic will look to you as the one man who can save them. Before reforming the Constitution – which is vital for you to do – you must first escape the murderous intentions of people close to you."

Laelius cried out in his sleep, causing our slumbering companions to groan loudly. I was almost ripped out of my dream.

"Be quiet," I murmured. "Please – let me stay in my dream."

My grandfather continued to speak as though there

had been no interruption.

"Reforming the Constitution for the good of the Republic is imperative, and if you do this you will be rewarded. Let me tell you now, Scipio, that every man who defends, expands or enriches the Republic, will be given a place in Heaven, where they may join their loved ones, and live with them in peace and happiness for all eternity.

"Nothing pleases the gods of the Universe more than seeing men coming together and being as one, united in one empire and under one set of common laws. The rulers of these states, though some may not even know it, are sent from Heaven to rule over their people, and will return to Heaven once their bodies die."

Despite the idea that for all the good deeds I'd done I might find my way to Heaven, I still felt uneasy – not because I was reminded of my mortality, but because someone close might kill me.

I asked my grandfather if, though his body was long dead, he was in fact still alive.

"Yes," he replied.

"And what about all those other people I had thought lost forever when they died – are they here now? What about my father?"

"Yes, Scipio," he smiled. "They are all here, alive and well. When their mortal bodies failed them, they were released from their Earthly chain and able to fly away to Heaven. Look, Scipio. See who is approaching. It is your father, Paulus!"

I turned and could scarcely believe my eyes. My father had come, and I was unable to hold back my tears. He embraced me, and kissed me, and told me to dry my eyes.

It was some time before I was able to stem the tearful flow, and after I had regained my composure I was just able to speak.

"Father, you were the best and noblest parent I could have wished for," I said.

He reciprocated the compliment, and I asked him, "If life on Earth is little more than death, while true life is here in Heaven among the ones I love, shouldn't I end my Earthly life as soon as I return there?"

My father shook his head.

"That is not the way of the Universe," he explained. "Unless the god of all that surrounds us releases you from your body, entry to this higher place will be forbidden. The same rule applies to all men. No one can hasten his own entry to Heaven by taking his own life. All men are made from those everlasting fires you call stars, spherical fires that orbit the Earth at great speed and each of which possesses its own divine intelligence, and all men are guardians of the globe that lies in the middle of the Heavens – the Earth. If you end your own life, you will be seen as deserting the post that was assigned to you. Only the god of all may decide how and when your mortal body shall die.

"While you are on Earth, you must be a man who is both pious and just, as I was, and your grandfather before me. The state will always take on the qualities of its people, and if you are noble and just, you will benefit the Republic. This then is the way into Heaven. Here you will be reunited those you loved and had once thought lost, in the place they call the Milky Way."

I gazed at all the Heavenly bodies that surrounded me, and among the fires of Heaven I saw a brilliant ring of light – the Milky Way.

I saw stars that could not be seen from Earth, and their size was almost beyond my comprehension. Of all the Heavenly bodies, the smallest was the Moon, reflecting the Sun's brilliant light. The Earth too was dwarfed by the stars, and suddenly man and all his follies and adventures and discoveries seemed insignificant. I suddenly felt embarrassed and ashamed that the Republic's mighty empire was an insignificant dot on a tiny planet.

My grandfather must have caught my gaze. "Come," he said. "Do not fixate upon the Earth. Let us look around the Heavens together."

He pointed and I followed the line of his finger. "See how the Universe is made of nine circles or, more accurately, nine spheres," he explained. "The outermost of these is the supreme deity embedded with stars, the Heavenly sphere that contains all others. Within this are seven spheres that orbit the Earth in contrary motion to the stars. The first sphere is Saturn, while the next, Jupiter, is a god-like place that gives hope and good health to mankind. Next is the Sun – ruler of all things luminous and is of such size that it gives everything in the system light. Next are Venus and Mercury, following the Sun as it moves. Last of all, and nearest the Earth, orbits the Moon, lit by the rays of the Sun.

While the Moon shall last forever, what lies beneath, on Earth, is doomed to wither and die. Only souls that the gods have given to mankind are eternal.

Earth, orbited by the planets and stars, lies at the heart of the Universe. It does not move, and all things of mass tend towards it."

I looked in awe at these immense globes as they orbited, and for the first time I was able to discern a sweet sound.

"What is that beautiful harmony that I can hear?" I asked.

"It is the sound of the planets," my father replied. "Each body in the Universe produces a sound, like a musical note, as it moves. Those objects furthest from the Earth produce higher notes, those closest produce the bass notes, and together they produce the most beautiful harmony."

"But I have never heard this sound before," I said, "and I have never read of it."

"There is no duller sense than that of hearing," said my father, "and men's ears, to some degree, have been deafened by this sound so they are unable to hear it."

The Heavens were a truly wondrous place, with the Moon and Sun, the planets and stars. But still, in spite of all the beauty and majesty of Heaven, I could not help but gaze once more towards the Earth.

"I see you are still thinking about the world that is your home," said my father. "When you return, and look back up into the night sky, you will realize how small and insignificant the Earth really is. It is only right you should think this, for it is the truth. You would also do well to realize, that compared to the size of the Earth, the Republic is barely a speck.

"Look Scipio. See how there are only a few pockets of civilization, surrounded by great swathes of emptiness. The size of these barren areas is so great that communication between these islands of civilization is impossible.

"If you seek glory, your fame might spread through the Republic – but for how long? The other pockets of human beings will never hear of you. Your fame will never be that great, when you look at the Earth as a whole. See how your planet is divided into zones white with ice in the north and south, a hot belt encompassing the middle of the Earth, and two habitable zones between the equator and each of the poles. Look at those men who inhabit the inhabitable zone in the south. They walk upside down, and their affairs will never concern you, and they will forever be oblivious to any so-called glory that you might achieve.

"If you climbed the Caucasus or swam across the Ganges, who beyond that tiny speck of an Empire would hear and celebrate your name? Ask yourself also for how long would your name be remembered? Your glory, like all glory, will surely fade away. To begin with, your children and grandchildren might celebrate all you have done, but in time your descendants will be as ignorant of your achievements as your ancestors.

"Just as the Republic is little more than a point on a small planet, so the time-scales you are familiar with are, in reality, fleeting moments. To you, a year is the time it takes for the Sun to return to its point of origin, but this is not quite so. A true year, a Heavenly measurement of time, occurs when all Heavenly bodies, stars and all, have gone through a full revolution and returned to their original points. How many generations come and go, I can scarcely imagine. Now you should have some sense of space and time on a cosmic scale."

"I understand," I replied. "Even if it is almost beyond my comprehension."

"If you wish to ascend to Heaven after your life ends," said my grandfather, "do not spend your life on Earth seeking out glory, or material possessions, or enslaving yourself to the opinions and whims of others. Do not be consumed by what others think and say about you. Rise above their cruel words. No matter how hard you try to appease them, they will always talk. Be pious, and just, and virtuous. These should be your aims while you walk the Earth, not so that you can get into Heaven, but because good deeds should be done for their own sake."

"Now that you have told me all this," I said, "I will try even harder to follow in your footsteps and those of my father. I hope I will fare well, and hope you will both be able to watch me from Heaven."

"Keep along the path you have already been following and you will not go wrong. Remember always that while your body will one day cease, your soul is immortal. You are a god Scipio; one that feels, acts and thinks, has memory and prescience, who is master of his physical body, just as the god of all moves the Universe.

"Spend your life in the pursuit of the noblest activities, doing what you can for your country, and putting others before yourself. Do this and your soul will be welcomed all the more into the Kingdom of

Heaven. Do not give yourself over to the pleasures of the flesh, and do not give in to whims and desires – this is to go against the laws of the gods and of fellow men. If you succumb to such temptations, your soul will spend many ages wandering unhappily upon the Earth, before finally being allowed into Heaven."

My grandfather faded before my very eyes, until he was nothing, and then I awoke from my dream.

True History

Lucian of Samosata

Introduction

Lucian of Samosata (125–c.180) was a Greek satirist of Syrian or Assyrian extraction, and *True History* is perhaps his most well-known tale. This piece of fantastical fiction parodies many works such as Homer's *Odyssey*, and is certainly a contender for the title of earliest science fiction story. In the first half of *True History*, the protagonist visits the Moon, meets extraterrestrial creatures, and takes part in interplanetary warfare.

In this second part the protagonist sails the ocean, visits strange islands, and meets Homer and Herodotus during his travels. In the end he tells of reaching a continent that he wishes to explore, and says he will relate his continuing adventures in a following volume. No such volume is known to exist, and so what happened to the character after this point is uncertain.

True History

Lucian of Samosata

Book 1

Athletes train on a regular basis, and no doubt look forward to taking a break from their exertions. Similarly, students who spend their time pouring over their academic texts, enjoy resting and thinking about more pleasurable things. While it might be tempting to spend time reading humorous texts, students might also wish to read something that is not only funny, but thought-provoking, and hopefully this book is just the thing.

I hope the readers will enjoy the humour and novelty of this book, and enjoy the lies that are woven together in what I hope is a believable way. I hope too that the reader will be amused by my parodies of poets, historians and philosophers.

No doubt the reader will recognize many of those whom I seek to imitate, but I will mention two of those whose work has influenced this book. Firstly I will mention Ctesias, who wrote fantastic tales about India without ever having been there. Secondly I wish to mention Iambulus who also wrote much that was untrue, but whose writings are all the more fun for the fantasies they contain.

Many have written of having visited lands that, in fact, do not exist, or at least do not exist outside their imaginations, and whose aim is to deceive gullible people. The man who first inspired this deceit was Homer's Odysseus, with his tales of one-eyed men, many-headed animals, cannibals, and the transformations of his drug-addled sailors. I do not blame people for writing such fantasies, but it does amaze me how they expect others to believe such blatant nonsense.

I have been eager for some time to write a story of my life, but my autobiography would make for a very dull read. So I have decided instead to do what many have done before, and write the most fantastic work of fiction my mind can create.

I shall differ from these other writers by acknowledging that everything I put to paper is nothing more than a series of lies. Nothing in this book is based on my life or the life of anyone I have known. It is a work of complete fiction, and no one should believe a word of what is written in this fantastical tale:

Many years ago, I began to wonder what land lay at the end of the Atlantic Ocean and, if such a place existed, what kind of strange beings might live there. At first this thought flitted idly through my mind, but soon this mild curiosity grew to something that continually gnawed at me, and in the end I felt compelled to seek out the answer myself.

I was fortunate enough to be the owner of a fine ship, and so had the means to satisfy my inquisitive mind. I filled the ship with plenty of fresh water, a good store of food, a great quantity of weapons, fifty crew whom I knew and trusted, and who shared my desire for adventure and knowledge, and I enlisted the finest sailing master money could induce.

We set forth across the Mediterranean, and with a fair wind behind us we passed through the Pillars of Hercules and out into the Atlantic Ocean. For the first day and night the wind calmed until there was not even the faintest gust. We barely travelled and looking back, the Pillars of Hercules remained quite visible.

On the second day however, the sun rose and brought with it a gale. The sea swelled, and dark clouds rushed towards us until they had blotted out the whole sky. The wind buffeted us mercilessly, and was so strong and so ferocious that we were unable to bring our sails in. At the mercy of the elements, we could do nothing but let ourselves be swept along, and for seventy nine helpless days the wind blew us across the ocean. On the eightieth day however, the storm abated, and the clouds broke up to reveal the sun once more.

With the darkness finally vanquished, I was able to make out a tree-covered island, some leagues away.

Still weak and weary from our months of hardship, we weighed anchor close to the shore, and rested ourselves on the beach. After lying on the sand for some hours, weary and miserable at our situation, I rose to my feet and commanded thirty crew to stay and guard our ship, while I led the rest of the crew on an expedition across the island.

We tramped into the wood, and after half a mile we

came to a clearing where we found a great slab of weathered bronze with an inscription. The writing was not altogether clear as the slab had turned green with age and the letters were faint or obliterated. After a careful examination, we were able to piece together the message:

"Hercules and Dionysus made it no further than this point" it read.

One of my men pointed out two giant sets of footprints, pressed deep in the earth. One must have been a hundred feet in length, and the other was smaller but still far beyond the size of an ordinary man. The larger print, I did not doubt, belonged to Hercules, and the smaller to Dionysus.

We gave our salutations to these two great beings, and continued with our exploration of the island. We had not had a drop to drink for so long that when we came across a river that cut through the wood, we knelt down gratefully and drank from it. To our surprise the river was not made of water, however, but of wine.

I decided to seek out the source of this strange river, and we followed it upstream. What we found were grapevines laden with fruit. From the roots of each vine came a stream of clear wine, and these streams came together to form the river.

Fish swam about under the surface, similar in colour to the wine. We caught and ate some of these fish and became drunk as a result, so we ate other fish we had brought with us on our expedition to mitigate the effects.

After eating, we pushed forwards once more, but

had not gone far when we came upon a wondrous sight. Some of the grapevines had trunks that were healthy and stout, but the upper part of each was a woman, perfectly formed from the waist up. Indeed, they reminded me of the pictures I had seen of Daphne turning into a tree just as Apollo catches her. The hair on each lady's head was made of leaves and tendrils, and from their fingertips grew branches full of grapes.

They welcomed us in a variety of languages; Indian and Lydian, but mostly Greek. They kissed some of my men on the lips, and those who were kissed instantly became drunk. The ladies would not let us take their fruit, and cried out in pain if we plucked a grape. Some of the women looked upon my men with hungry eyes, and asked if my crew might embrace them. Two men ventured forward and wrapped their arms about these strange creatures, but the moment they did so they found themselves stuck; their lower bodies had grown thick roots, their hair had turned to leaves and tendrils, and they were already beginning to bear fruit like the women.

Nothing could be done to break this strange spell so, leaving our two unfortunate men, we returned to the ship and recounted our adventure to the rest of the crew. We filled barrels with fresh water and wine from the island, and camped on the beach overnight.

As the sun rose and was barely above the horizon, we boarded our ship and set sail. The wind picked up with every hour, and I heard a crew member shout fearfully and point. In the distance a waterspout rose from the sea and reached high into the sky, far above any clouds. In a restless manner it twisted and bent, and moved towards us in a most ominous manner.

I called for the crew to set sail away as quickly as possible from this phenomenon, but it gained ground with every minute, until at last we were lashed by its watery coil and we were forced to brace ourselves. The boat was sucked upwards, mile after mile. For seven days and nights we sailed through the sky and through a fog of clouds until, at last, we were let down on a strange land that was bright and round and shining a brilliant light.

Surveying the landscape, there were islands and water, and we soon saw that the islands were inhabited and cultivated. In the sky we say great flying creatures heading towards us, and as they approached, we saw that they were men flying on three-headed vultures. The great birds landed in front of us and the men dismounted. They said they were the king's Vulture Soldiers, and told us that we were all under arrest. The leader of the Vulture Soldiers explained that it was the job of his men to fly about the country and bring any strangers they might find to the court of the king.

We were escorted to the king's palace where the king surveyed us all curiously, not least the clothes we wore.

"You are Greeks, are you not?" he said.

"We are," I replied.

He looked at me puzzled, and shook his head. "How did you get here – when there is nothing but air between our two worlds?"

"A waterspout whipped up my boat," I explained. "It carried us for seven days and seven nights before depositing us here."

The king nodded. "My name is Endymion," he said, "and I too am from your country. I was brought here in a dream and was made king of this world that by night shines down upon your Earth. You are standing on the Moon."

He pointed through a window, and in the night sky we saw a world with rivers and seas, forests and mountains and cities. It was our world, Earth.

"You have no need to fear us," said the king. "You are in no danger, and I will ensure all your needs are met. And if I am victorious in my war with the people of the Sun, then you can share in my success and lead the happiest of lives in my world."

"Who are these people of the Sun?" I asked. "And why do you fight them?"

"Years ago," said the king, "I decided to gather together the poorest people on my world, and use them to set up a colony on Venus – a world that is currently uninhabited. But Phaethon, King of the Sun, sent his Ant Soldiers out to thwart our colonization. We were forced to retreat, for we were no match for them. But now we are stronger, and I desire to make war with the people of the Sun, and again establish a colony on Venus. If you wish, you and your men can join me in battle. I will give you a uniform and a royal vulture, and we shall set off together tomorrow."

I nodded. "My men and I will join you."

We stayed the night as guests of the king, and noticed that there were no women upon the Moon, only men, and indeed the king confirmed this. I would have asked many questions, but my men and I needed to rest, so we slept as best we could, and the next morning we prepared for battle.

My men and I, seated on our vultures, took our place among the strangest array of creatures. There were eighty thousand mounted Vulture Soldiers; there were birds with grass plumage and lettuce-leaf wings; there were giant fleas that had travelled from the Great Bear constellation with archers on their backs, and a host of other fabulous beasts.

Giant spiders, the size of islands, were told by the king to weave a web between the Moon and Venus. What the spiders actually wove was a thick plane extending like a bridge between both worlds, and some sixty million men were deployed on it.

All the soldiers, including myself, were attired with armour made from lupine skins, helmets hollowed out from tough beans, and we were given swords and shields emblazoned with Greek patterns.

A scout warned that the enemy was approaching, and sure enough we saw Phaethon, King of the Sun, coming towards us with his equally strange army. There were some fifty thousand Ant Soldiers, each ant being some two hundred feet long; fifty thousand archers mounted on giant mosquitoes; beings who fired deadly radishes; Mushroom Men who used mushrooms as shields and asparaguses as spears, and dog-faced men who had flown from the Dog Star on winged acorns. The Sun King was supposed to have been joined by the formidable Cloud Centaurs, but as the enemy approached us the Cloud Centaurs were nowhere to be seen. Finally there were the donkeys who began to bray, and so signalled the start of the battle.

The Vulture Soldiers, myself included, rushed forwards only to see the whole of the Sun King's left flank flee. We pursued them without letting up, until at last we caught them and were able to cut them down.

Their right flank faired much better, with their mosquitoes very much on the offensive. Only when our infantry joined the battle did the mosquitoes finally retreat, and when they saw their left flank had been annihilated, they turned and fled.

It was a swift and glorious victory. We took many prisoners, and an even greater number were slain. So much blood poured onto the clouds beneath us that they turned crimson, just like when the sun sets. Indeed, I wonder if this is what happened when, as Homer mentioned, after the death of Sarpedon, Zeus turned the rain into blood.

All the soldiers of the Moon King celebrated routing the enemy. The infantry celebrated upon the giant spider web, while the rest of us who had fought in the great sky battle alighted on clouds and bathed in our victory.

Our celebrations were premature. Scouts came to us in a state of panic – the Cloud Centaurs who had not arrived to help the King of the Sun before battle were now fast approaching. I looked up and saw shapes, indistinct at first, approaching at great speed. Most of the Moon King's men had not even noticed the spectacle, and we were ill-prepared for another fight. The Cloud Centaurs were a sight to behold. They were winged horses, but with the upper bodies of men. These were massive creatures – from the waist up each man was as large as the Colossus of Rhodes.

Their leader was the Archer from the Zodiac, and when they saw their allies had been defeated, they sent word to Phaethon telling him to advance again. Before the people of the Moon were able to regroup for battle, the Cloud Centaurs swooped down and attacked. The Moon King's soldiers were either slain or put to flight, and even those who fled were caught and cut down. Endymion, the King of the Moon, was pursued back to the Moon's capital, where most of his birds were killed. My men and I were chased across the spider's web, and I was captured along with two of my companions.

Our hands were tied behind our backs, bound by thread from the spiders' web, and we were taken to the Sun. The Sun King decided not to lay siege to the Moon, but instead to build a wall in the air so that the rays of the Sun should no longer reach the Moon. The Wall was not made of stone, but of cloud, and the Moon was completely shrouded in darkness.

Endymion sent a message to Phaethon, begging the King of the Sun to tear down the wall and let the Moon be flooded with light once more. In return for this, the King of the Moon promised to pay the King of the Sun money in perpetuity, to become an ally of the Sun People, never to make war again, and suggested they swap all the hostages that they had captured.

At first Phaethon and his Sun People were still incensed by the war-like ways of Endymion and the People of the Moon, and they would not countenance any sort of treaty. But, in time, their feelings and their position softened, and they sent the Moon People their terms for peace:

The People of the Sun and their allies shall make a treaty with the People of the Moon, under the following conditions:

– Each world shall exchange all prisoners captured during their war

– The Sun People shall pull down the wall of cloud that blocks the light to the Moon

– The Sun People shall never again invade the Moon

– The Moon People shall never invade the Sun

– Each world shall aid the other if either one comes under attack

– The Moon People shall allow all stars and planets to remain autonomous

– The King of the Moon shall send the King of the Sun ten thousand gallons of dew as tribute, and give ten thousand of his men over as hostages

– The colonization of Venus shall be carried out concurrently by both the Moon People and the Sun People, and any others who wish to do so

– This treaty shall be inscribed on a slab that will be positioned equidistantly between worlds

The treaty was signed by three officials from the Sun and three from the Moon, and on these terms peace was made. The cloud-wall was dismantled and my two men and I, who were still prisoners, were released and allowed to return to the Moon.

When we reached our destination, Endymion himself greeted us, as did our old crew mates who wept with happiness.

Endymion, who was overjoyed at our return, kindly offered me his son's hand in marriage. He could not persuade me however, and in the end he had to accept my decision. I asked him that I be allowed to return to my homeland, along with my crew. Endymion reluctantly agreed, but he asked me to stay another week, which I did.

Those days were among the strangest I can recount, such are the ways of the People of the Moon. There are no women on the Moon, and they had not even heard of the word. It is a place where men marry men, and men give birth to children. Before the age of twenty-five men act as wives, and thereafter they assume the role of husband.

I saw that pregnant men did not carry their unborn babies in their stomachs, but in their calves. Conception does not take place as one might expect – instead each man has a hole in the hollow of his knee. After the act, the man's calf will gradually begin to swell, until the baby is ready for delivery. When it is due, the calf is cut and the baby is taken out, quite dead, then a Moon Person will gently breathe life into the baby's mouth.

If this sounds unusual then I shall tell you another

way they go about procreating that is even more fantastic. They have beings called Arboreals who are brought about through a most unusual process. A man's right testicle is cut off, and then planted in the ground. Over time it grows into a large tree made of flesh. It is shaped like a giant phallus, and when I first saw such a tree, it reminded me of the tale of Priapus. The tree has branches and leaves, and eventually bears fruit in the form of giant acorns. When the fruit eventually ripen, they are harvested. Men cut them down from the trees, slice them open, and inside the giant acorns are the men who, as already mentioned, are called Arboreals.

Another unusual aspect with regards Moon People, is that they have artificial phalluses. The rich have phalluses of ivory or other expensive materials, while the poor generally have phalluses of wood which are used during intercourse.

When a man grows old and dies, he does not become a corpse, instead he gradually turns to vapour and becomes at one with the air.

All Moon People eat the same food, namely frogs. These amphibians do not hop around but instead fly through the air, and are caught and cooked on hot coals. While the frogs are roasting, the natives sit about the fire and inhale the smoke that rises, before finally consuming their meal.

Their favoured drink is also very peculiar – it is the air, which is quite liquid and is squeezed into cups like dew. They also never need to relieve themselves and they do not have the necessary bodily parts to do so.

Any man on the Moon is considered beautiful if he

has not the slightest scrap of hair on his head, and any person with long hair is reckoned to be quite hideous. People who live on comets, however, hold the opposite view, and consider anyone with long hair to be quite beautiful.

Moon People have a great number of unusual aspects to their bodies, which are quite dissimilar to our own. Adult Moon People have beards that grow not from their chins, but from their knees. They have only one toe on each foot, and no toenails. Each man has a cabbage-leaf tail that hangs and covers his buttocks, and never breaks even if he falls on his behind. When their noses run, honey of great pungency pours from their nostrils. When they work hard or take exercise, milk sweats from their bodies. The milk is of such quality that, with the addition of a little honey, it can be made into a quite delicious cheese.

They use their bellies as pockets, and can open and shut these pouches. Inside their bellies there appear to be no intestines, instead I have only ever noticed hair, and during colder periods the children are able to climb into these pouches and keep warm.

If I tell you the amazing properties of their eyes, you will most probably think I am a very great liar. Nevertheless, I shall take that risk:

Their eyes are not fixed in their skulls, but can be plucked out of their sockets. If they have no need to see anything, they frequently take their eyes out and stow them away. Then, when the need arises, they retrieve their eyes and put them back in. If a person should happen to lose his own eyes, he will simply borrow another person's so that he can see once more. The wealthier class of people always keep a large stock of eyes.

The Moon's citizens generally have leaves for ears. Those who do not are the Arboreals who instead have ears made of wood.

From onions they extract oil which is clear and sweet-smelling like myrrh. They have water-grapes that resemble hailstones. When the wind blows, the grapevines are shaken, and the result is that these hailstones come loose and tumble down to Earth.

When it comes to clothes, the rich wear garments made from a soft and malleable glass, while the poor wear clothes spun from bronze, which is first turned into a wool-like substance by soaking it in water.

I was walking across the royal grounds when I came across a large, angled mirror, fixed above a well. I was told that any person looking into the mirror can see every country and every city on Earth, just as if he was flying over it. If a person descends this shallow well they can hear every word that is spoken on the planet below.

I peered into this strange looking-glass, and was able to see my family and my native land, though I am unable to say if they were able to see me.

I know I have made an astonishing series of claims, but any doubter, if he reaches the Moon himself, will know that I am speaking the truth.

So these seven days of observing the Moon and the people who lived there passed, and it was time for me and my men to bid farewell to the king and the other Moon People whom we had befriended.

Endymion gave me two tunics made of glass, five of bronze, and a suit of lupine armour. These gifts and more were placed on our ship, and we set sail from the Moon, escorted some sixty miles by a thousand Vulture Soldiers. After they left us and returned to the Moon, we passed many places on our voyage, but we did not stop until we reached Venus. The world was already being colonized by people from the Moon and the Sun. We rested there awhile, and filled our barrels with their water.

We returned to our ship and set off once more, travelling towards the Zodiac. Our journey took us past the Sun. Many of the crew wished to pay a visit to the Sun, but owing to unfavourable winds we were sadly unable. We did at least pass close enough by to see that the lands were green and lush and well kept. Something we hadn't bargained for however were the Cloud Centaurs, who on seeing us flew up towards our ship. Without the Vulture Soldiers protection, I feared there might be another bloody battle. Fortunately we were able to head off any skirmish by showing them the peace treaty, and the Cloud Centaurs left us in peace.

Sailing for another night and day, beginning our slow descent to Earth, we came across a city floating between the constellations of Pleiades and Hyades. This was the City of Light. We landed and toured the town. Here we found no men, only flaming torches. We saw them running down streets, relaxing in the public square, or waiting down at the harbour. Some torches were small and scruffy, while a few were large, powerful and conspicuous.

Each torch had his own house or sconce, each torch had his own name, and we even heard them talking. As a gesture of goodwill we were invited into their homes, but we were distrustful of them and we neither ate a morsel that was offered to us, or slept the night.

In the centre of their city, there was a public building, where the city's judge sat. He would call each torch by name, and any torch that did not answer his call was sentenced to death for desertion. The method of execution was by extinguishing. My crew and I even visited the court and watched the proceedings. Here we saw torches defending themselves, and explaining why they had come so late.

It was in the court that I came across a familiar figure – my own flaming torch. We talked for a while, and he told me about his home life.

After this fleeting reunion, my crew and I returned to the ship and set off once more. Again we found ourselves floating across the Earth's sky, and slowly downwards, until we were as low as the clouds. There was a city on one of the clouds but, as happened when we passed the Sun, the wind prevented us from paying the Cloud City a visit. As I looked down at the clouds I could not help but be reminded of Aristophanes' great play.

After another two days the ocean was in plain sight, but the only place we could land, given we were still high in the air, were floating lands that seemed fiery and bright.

Finally, the wind fell to a gentle breeze and we were able to touch down on the ocean. The weather was fine and the sea was calm, and in their happiness and excitement to have returned from our aerial travels the crew leapt overboard and swam happily in the water.

Unfortunately, it is often the case that a time of happiness is followed quickly by one of misery:

For two days we sailed in fair weather, and it was on the third day that one of the crew spotted a number of sea-monsters. The creatures were whales, the largest of which was a hundred and fifty miles long. As this mighty beast pushed towards us, his gargantuan mouth open, we had no chance of escape. Before he had reached us, the water he was displacing caused our ship to be thrown about violently, and turned much of the ocean to foam.

Every person on the boat believed himself doomed. We embraced and said our last goodbyes, and waited for death.

The monster's teeth were larger than great statues, white as ivory, and sharper than the jagged metal spines of caltrops. The water that the whale was swallowing pulled us unstoppably between his teeth, and then his mouth snapped shut, just missing our boat and leaving us in complete darkness.

We were thankful that we should still be alive, but our our ordeal was clearly not over. After some time in this dark void, the whale opened his mouth once more, and we were able to survey our surroundings.

We were in something resembling a great, domed cavern, large enough to house a great city. All about us there was water with all sorts of detritus floating about: there were the remains of fish both large and small, there was ships' rigging, anchors, merchandise, human bones, and the remains of creatures that I could not recognize.

In the middle of this great artificial lake was an island which, I imagine, had formed over time from all the mud the whale had swallowed. Trees had grown and covered much of the island, there were plants, and there was life, and it seemed clear to me that the island had been cultivated by intelligent minds.

We sailed about the coast of the island and found it to be twenty-seven miles in circumference. We also saw a great variety of birds in the trees, including seagulls and kingfishers.

When we weighed anchor and went ashore, many of my men could not help but cry and lament our miserable situation. I tried to rouse the crew, and suggested we light a fire to banish the darkness. We still had fish on board our ship, and we also had plenty of water that we had brought with us from Venus. After gathering what dry wood we could find, and rubbing two sticks together we were soon able to cook some fish over a blazing fire.

We slept soundly, and on waking the next day we were able to see the outside world in glimpses whenever the whale opened his great mouth. We might see mountains, then endless sky, and then islands, and we reasoned that he must be moving swiftly through the ocean.

As we were unsure if we would ever be able to escape from within this great beast, I took seven of my men into the forest, which I wished to explore. We had travelled close to a mile when, obscured by trees, we came across a temple. An inscription told us it had been dedicated to Poseidon, and on exploring the grounds around the temple we found a number of graves.

But there were livelier signs too. Nearby, there was a spring of clear water. In the distance we heard a dog barking, and venturing in that direction we first saw smoke, and then a farmhouse.

We made our way to the house, and saw a boy and an old man, hard at work watering their garden. They saw us but at first said nothing and we all stood in silence.

At last the old man spoke: "Who are you, strangers? Are you sea-gods, or unlucky men like us?"

"We are men," I replied.

The old man nodded. "We too are men, born on land. But given our situation we have become sea-creatures and swim with the creatures that surround our island. Sometimes I wonder if we now reside in the land of the dead, but sincerely hope that we are still alive."

"You are alive, sir," I reassured. "My men and I were swallowed, ship and all, by this great beast only yesterday. We came ashore on this island and decided to explore the forest and now, by some good fortune, have met other men who share our predicament in being imprisoned inside this whale. Pray tell us who you are and how you came to be trapped here like us."

But on both these points the old man remained silent, and beckoned us to follow him into his house.

His home was spacious and comfortable; there were bunk beds, and all sorts of other furniture. We sat ourselves down at a table, and the host laid out a meal of fish and fruit and vegetables, and poured us all goblets full of wine.

At last he spoke, but not of himself. "Tell me of your adventures that led you here."

I spoke at length of the storm that had blown us to the island with the strange female vines, of our trip to the Moon and the battles between the people of the Moon and of the Sun, and all the rest up to our being swallowed by the whale.

Our host was amazed by our adventures, and then he recounted his own tale:

"My name is Scintharus. I have not always lived in this great beast. Originally I hale from Cyprus. My boy, Cinyras, who is with us now, my servants, and I set sail from our native country in the hope of trading in Italy. For much of the journey our voyage was a pleasant one. But as we neared Sicily, the wind picked up and drove us far out into the ocean. It was during this storm that we were swallowed by the whale. Our ship was smashed and the only people to survive were myself and my son.

"We buried what crew happened to be washed up onto this island, and we built a temple to Poseidon, and live here now, surviving on vegetables and fish and nuts. The forest also contains many grape-vines, from which we derive our delicious wine, and we also have the spring that you no doubt saw.

"Our beds are made of leaves, we have more than enough wood to burn fires, and the fish and birds are plentiful in number and easy enough to catch. There is also a lake not too far from here. It's a few miles in circumference, with all kinds of fish swimming about under the surface. It's also a lovely place to swim, and

I have a small boat which my son and I use to sail.

"Twenty seven years have passed since we were swallowed, and our lives here would have been a tolerable one – if it was not for our neighbours."

My mouth dropped open. "You mean there are other people inside the whale?"

"Yes," Scintharus said grimly. "There are lots of them. But they are all unpleasant and quarrelsome. In the western part of the forest live the Lobster Men. They have eel-eyes, and faces like lobsters. They love nothing more than to pick a fight with anyone. There are also Fish Men who have the upper bodies of men and the lower bodies of catfish, and a host of other creatures that resemble both humans and sea creatures. I am forced to pay the tribute of five hundred oysters a year to some of these creatures, but I'm tired of it – it is no life."

I pitied the poor man and told him as much.

"Do you think," he asked, "that we might be able to wage war on these creatures? I have no doubt if they find out about you – which no doubt they will – they will expect tribute from you too."

"How many of them are there?" I asked.

"More than a thousand," Scintharus replied.

"What sort of weapons do they have?"

"Nothing at all, but for a few fish bones."

"Good," I said. "I think we have some chance. Hopefully they are unaware of our existence. We should meet them in battle, and quickly. We have superior weapons, and we will have the element of surprise."

The old man was heartened by my words, and I

went on:

"If we defeat them, then we can live out the rest of our lives in peace."

Our plan was to draw the enemy to us, rather than blunder into their territory of which we knew little. To this end, Scintharus did not pay the tribute when the time came, and a messenger was sent by one of the Fish Men demanding that the payment of five hundred oysters be made at once. Scintharus gave the messenger a contemptuous reply and chased him off.

The following day they sent some of their men to attack Scintharus and his son, but we were lying in wait and were able to cut the men down with ease. We chased after the few that escaped and followed them back to their den. After a short and glorious battle, we found ourselves victorious. The number of their dead was a hundred and seventy five, and the number of our dead was just one – our sailing-master, who had been run through with a sharpened fish-bone.

We celebrated through the night, but the next morning more of their men were sent and they knew now that there was more than just a man and his son to deal with. We met them outside the temple of Poseidon. Again we were able to rout them; their weapons were simply no match for ours, and, as before, we chased the enemy into the forest. This time they knew they were well and truly beaten, and now it was we, and not they, who were rulers of this island.

They sent men to take away their dead, and sent a party to discuss the formation of an alliance. We, however, thought it best not to engage in any sort of treaty and, the next day, we marched into their territory and killed every one of them – except for the Sea Goats who fled the scene and hurled themselves into the sea.

With the enemy vanquished or killed, we were all able to live in peace. It was a luxurious life in many ways where we were able to spend our time in leisurely pursuits such as hunting, sports, tending vines and gathering fruit. But for all this life of idle pleasure, it still troubled me that we were ultimately prisoners, cut off from the outside world by this great whale.

For a year and eight months we lived this life. But early during our ninth month, not long after the whale opened it's mouth, as it did on a regular basis, we heard a commotion. I heard what sounded like the drum-beats that sailors row to, and with my men I crossed the island towards the opening of the whale's mouth, and peered towards the outside world.

What we saw, we could scarcely believe. Huge men were rowing islands that were miles in circumference, using cypress trees as oars. The trees that covered the island had large leaves which together had the combined effect not dissimilar to a boat's sail.

At first there were only two or three, but soon more came into sight until I counted over six hundred islands. Their intentions soon became clear when some collided head-on, and a number were scuttled and sunk. The giants sometimes ran aboard an enemy's island and hand-to-hand battles took place. No quarter was given.

They struck at one another with massive oysters and with giant sponges. From what we were able to discern, the battle stemmed from one sides act of piracy, where herds of dolphins belonging to the other side were driven off. Eventually the victims of this piracy were the victors in battle, and the other side fled.

The remaining giants, tethered their islands to the whale, and were pulled along for the next day, before burying their fallen friends on the whale, then sailing away on their strange islands until they were beyond the horizon.

Book 2

I had become accustomed to living inside the whale, but upon seeing the outside world once more I felt discontented with this life and sought a way of escape. Our first attempt involved digging through the side of the whale, but after tunnelling more than half a mile we gave up. Our next plan was to set the forest alight and hopefully kill the whale. For a week we worked night and day, setting the forest ablaze, beginning near the tail, but it was only on the eighth and ninth days that the whale showed any symptoms of illness. He yawned less frequently, and his yawns did not last as long. On the tenth and eleventh days, we knew that the fires were really having an effect, and he made the most tremendous noises.

On the twelfth day we realized that if we did not prop open his mouth the next time he yawned, we might find ourselves stuck inside a dead whale and die there ourselves. Some crew took trees to the whale's mouth and waited. When he yawned, his mouth was propped open.

With Scintharus as our new sailing-master, we filled our boat with what provisions we were able to gather. One more day passed before the whale died, and we set off in our boat, making our way between the creature's teeth with some difficulty.

For three days we camped on the whale's back, and on the fourth day we set off in our boat. We sailed between the bodies of the dead giants, and upon measuring their bodies were amazed at their height.

We travelled in a northerly direction and as each day passed the climate cooled. Then, after a week of sailing, the north wind brought with it a great chill. The temperature plunged so much that the sea froze over, and our boat lay on top of a great sheet of ice that spread all about us as far as the eye could see.

The wind was so cold, we were barely able to stand it. Scintharus proposed that we dig a hole in the ice so that we might be sheltered from the chilly gusts. So we did, and we hid away. But we could not stay there for ever, and after thirty days our provisions ran out. So we returned to our boat which had frozen to the ice, and dug it out. Boarding and spreading out the canvas sails, we found the boat sailed across the ice as easily as travelling across water. For five days we endured both cold and hunger, until the weather grew milder, the ice broke up, and at the sea turned to water once more.

After sailing for forty miles, we reached a desert island where we were able to replenish our water supplies, and were able to kill two wild bulls, that had horns not on their heads but under their eyes.

Further on the sea turned to milk, and within this strange sea we spied a white island full of grapevines. The island was made of cheese and was some three miles in circumference, while the grapes yielded not wine but milk.

In the middle of the island was a temple, built in honour of Galatea the Nereid. We stayed on the island for five days, using it as our bread and meat, and using the grapes to quench our thirst.

Returning to our boat and departing, the sea slowly changed over three days from milk back to water. Two days later, as we sailed the blue sea, we saw men running across the water's surface. They were like other men in every way, but for their feet which were made of cork. Some bounded over the waves to see us, and greeted us in Greek. They were friendly, and talked to us at length, telling us they were on their way to their capital city, which was also called Cork. For some time they jogged alongside our boat, until they had to turn off, but not before wishing us good luck.

A number of islands came into sight, one of which was made entirely of cork, and there we watched the Cork-Men step ashore. The other islands, five in total, were some way off. Soon we noticed many small fires blazing upon them. The nearest was low-lying and rather flat. As we neared, we could smell a sweet fragrance wafting through the air. The aroma was a mixture of many blooms: roses, violets, lilies and more.

There were woods filled with songbirds, and we could hear pleasant music. It seemed, from what we could hear, that there was a party with people singing and playing instruments. It was so pleasantly intoxicating that we anchored our boat in one of the island's many harbours and went ashore, leaving Scintharus and two sailors aboard.

Advancing through the woodland, we came across some guards who bound us with rose-wreaths and escorted us further inland. As we walked, the guards told us that we were being taken to their leader and that we would have to await our trial. We were fourth in line to face the ruler's judgement, and as we awaited our turn we watched the three preceding trials.

The first case involved Ajax, son of Telamon, who was accused of having turned mad. The judgement was given and Ajax was finally put in the care of Hippocrates, the physician, until he had recovered his wits.

The second trial was to decide if Helen should live with Theseus or Menelaus. After much argument, it was decided that she should live with Menelaus, as he has suffered much to be with her, and Theseus already had a number of wives.

The third case was to determine whether Alexander the Great, outranked Hannibal, and in the end it was decided that this was indeed so.

When we were put on trial we were asked how we had come to the Island of the Blessed while still alive. Only dead heroes were allowed here. We told them of our entire adventure, and then the ruler consulted some of those who were close to him, before pronouncing his verdict. We were told that as we were still alive, they could not try us, and that we were to return there after death for our trial.

For seven months they let us stay with them, before we were taken to a great city of gold and emerald. The gates, seven in all, were of cinnamon, and the ground was pure ivory, while around the city was a river of myrrh.

Within, the residents had no visible form. They bathed in hot dew, heated by burning cinnamon, and wore clothes made of fine, purple spider-webs. We knew of their existence, by their clothes and by the fact that they moved and talked. They were souls, and reminded me of upright shadows, though completely invisible rather than black.

No one there grew old, and similarly the island perpetually hovered around dawn, or perhaps dusk, in permanent gloom. There was also only one continuous season, that of spring, and everywhere was in constant bloom. The fruit trees yielded fruit thirteen times each year, while the grape vines produced grapes once a month. Within the city, there were three hundred and sixty-five water springs, and other springs of honey and of myrrh, and there were also seven milk rivers, and eight wine rivers.

Outside the city was a great table, where the city's inhabitants would often gather. Nearby were glass trees that bore not fruit but cups, and the inhabitants were attended by the winds. Anyone who put a cup on the table would see it fill at once with wine.

Here they sang and recited poetry, usually the works of Homer, who sometimes joined the table. They were also accompanied in song by choruses of boys and girls, and choruses of birds singing from within the woodland.

As well as the springs already mentioned, two others ran close to the table, one filled with laughter and the other with enjoyment. Everyone at the table drank from these as soon as they arrived and so enjoyed themselves and laughed heartily throughout their meal.

While I was there I also met many demigods and legendary heroes. Present were both Cyruses, the Scythian Anacharsis, the divine being Zamolxis, and

Numa Pompilius, the successor of Romulus. In addition, there were Lycurgus of Sparta, Phocion, Tellus of Athens, and, but for Periander of Corinth, all the wise men. I also saw Socrates debating with Nestor and Palamedes. While close to them were Hyacinth of Sparta, Narcissus of Thespiae, Hylas and a host of other great figures.

Socrates seemed to favour Hyacinth above all others, for Hyacinth was someone he happily disagreed with more than anyone else. The wise king of this island, and Judge of the Dead, Rhadamanthus was constantly irritated by Socrates and his self-righteous ways, and Rhadamanthus repeated his threats to banish Socrates from the island unless he became less serious and more jolly.

Plato, the famous student of Socrates, was not there, and it was said that he was living in an imaginary city, that was answerable to the laws and constitution that he himself had written.

Aristippus, Epicurus and their many followers, were held in high regard by many of the heroes, because of their amiable natures. Aesop the great teller of fables was there also, in the role of a jester.

Diogenes the famous Cynic, was there too, but he was a changed man. Instead of criticising everyone and everything, he married Lais the courtesan, and spent most of his time dancing or carrying out silly pranks.

None of the Stoics were there. It was said that they were still journeying up the steep path of virtue. The Academicians had been invited to come to the Island of the Blessed, but they could not cease their debating and take any practical steps. Indeed, one of the topics they debated was the very existence of the island. I imagine too that they feared Rhadamanthus would pass an unfavourable judgement upon them. It was said that some Academicians, had set off for the island, but being unable to agree on just about anything, they only made it half-way before turning back.

The islanders' attitude towards relationships is very open, and they will do any manner of things in public that most would rather keep indoors. Socrates claimed that he had never had relationships with young ladies, but on this matter he was found by everyone to be guilty of perjury. All the men shared their wives with one another, and no one was jealous of other people's relationships.

After a few days, I met Homer, and decided to ask him about his past.

"It's often been debated which part of the world you come from," I said. "Some say you are from Ithica, some say you are from Smyrna, and others say you are from Chios. Could you answer that question once and for all?"

"I am from Babylon," he replied. "My name was Tigranes, but when I was captured by the Greeks and held hostage – or as a Greek like you might also say *homeros* – I changed my name.

"Why did you begin the Iliad with Achilles being in such a state of anger?"

"It just came into my mind that way. The idea wasn't taken from anyone or anywhere else."

"Which of your two great works did you write

first?"

"You mean the Iliad or the Odyssey?"

I nodded. "Most scholars seem to think you wrote the Odyssey first."

"Then they are wrong."

One question I wanted answered was whether or not, as legend had it, he was blind. But I did not have to ask, for it was clear enough that he could see.

I met with Homer many times, and he was happy to answer my many questions. I even broached the delicate matter of when Thersites had accused him of libel. It is true that Thersites had been ridiculed in the Iliad, but with Odysseus as his lawyer, Homer eventually won the case.

While I was there, the mathematician and philosopher, Pythagoras arrived. During his life, his soul had lived in seven bodies and had now ended its migration. The right hand side of his body was made entirely of gold, and after some discussion it was eventually agreed that he could join the Island of the Blessed.

Empedocles came too, his body burned after he perished in Mount Etna, but unlike Pythagoras, and despite his many protests, he was not allowed to stay.

One of the highlights of my stay were the Games of the Dead, with Achilles and Theseus acting as referees. The first competition was wrestling, and Caranus, descendant of Hercules, defeated Odysseus in the final. In the boxing, the final was a draw between Areius and Epeius. I do not remember who won the sprint, but in poetry Hesiod won, even though Homer's writings were far better. Each person who won was awarded a crown adorned with peacock feathers.

To this point, my stay had been a happy one, but it was not to last. Not long after the games, we heard that those who had been imprisoned on the Island of the Wicked had managed to overcome their guards and had set sail for the Island of the Blessed.

Those who had escaped included the tyrant Phalaris of Acragas, Busiris the Egyptian, Diomedes of Thrace, the robber Sciron and the bandit Sinis.

Rhadamanthus gathered together all the heroes on the shore, led by Theseus, Achilles, and Ajax, who had now recovered his wits.

The battle was not long and the heroes soon overcame the invaders. Achilles contributed the greatest amount to their success, but Socrates too exceeded himself, putting up a far better fight than when he had fought at Delium. Even when four of the enemy charged at him, he stood firm. In return for his bravery, Socrates was given a park of his own. Here he was able to gather people around him and engage in debate. These grounds he named the Academy of the Dead.

The defeated army of wicked men were clasped in irons and sent back to their island, where they were to be punished more severely than before. Homer wrote a poem celebrating the victory, and when I later left the island he gave me a copy of the poem which I unfortunately lost. It was also by no means the end of the islanders' troubles.

Cinyras, the son of Scintharus, and an able member of our crew, was a tall, handsome youth who had fallen in love with Menelaus's wife, Helen. It seemed that her romantic feelings for him were even stronger. They often winked and smiled at one another at the table, and they would often go for walks together in the wood.

One day Cinyras and Helen desired to make love, and decided it would be best if they first went to another island. Few people knew of this plan, namely three of my crew who were needed to escort them. Cinyras and Helen feared that Cinyras's father, Scintharus, might find out, for they knew that he was against them having any sort of relationship.

It was late at night when they set off, and most people, including myself, were fast asleep. Helen's husband, Menelaus woke up and upon seeing that his wife was not at his side, caused a great commotion and took his brother with him to see King Rhadamanthus.

When day broke, some lookouts spotted a ship near the horizon, and when the news was passed to King Rhadamanthus, he put fifty men aboard a ship carved from a single log and ordered them to chase down the distant ship.

At noon, just as Helen and Cinyras were entering into the milky waters, on their way to the Island of Cheese, they were caught and escorted home. Helen wept and locked herself in her room filled with shame, while Cinyras and the three other crewmen who had helped him were banished to the Island of the Wicked.

Tainted by association, and for not keeping my men under my control, I, along with the rest of my crew were to spend only one more day on the island before having to leave.

To my shame, I began to cry and weep. I did not want to leave this wondrous place. Many of those that I had befriended tried to cheer me up and reassure me. They told me I would return there again one day, and that my seat was already prepared, and situated close to the best people.

I turned to Rhadamanthus and asked him what my future held.

"You will have a good many adventures before you return to your native land."

"And when will I return to my home?"

But Rhadamanthus did not answer, instead he pointed out to sea, where an island was emitting many plumes of smoke. "That," he said, "is the Island of the Wicked. Nearby I'm sure you can see another four islands, and there in the distance you should be able to see another island."

I nodded.

"That," said Rhadamanthus, "is the Island of Dreams. Further still, and some way out of sight, is the island of Ogygia. When you have sailed past all these islands, you will come to a great continent opposite the one you inhabit."

He picked a mallow root and handed it to me.

"When you are faced with any great danger, pray to this root," he said. "When you reach the great continent, do not eat lupines, do not stoke fires with the blade of your sword, and never make love to anyone over the age of eighteen. Heed these words and you will one day return to this island."

On the day that my crew and I were due to leave, and we walked down to the harbour, I saw that Homer had carved a couplet, dedicated to me, on a slab of polished beryl:

Lucian

Mistrusted at first, but now departs,
Forever remembered in all our hearts.

My crew and I readied ourselves to set sail. Odysseus, without the knowledge of his wife, Penelope, handed me a letter and asked me to take it to Calypso on the Island of Ogygia. Rhadamanthus sent Nauplius, son of Poseidon, to escort us for the first few leagues, so that none of the islanders would suspect us of any untoward motives.

After a few hours of sailing, the fresh breeze that filled my lungs with excitement was soon replaced by a most awful stench. I could smell burning sulphur and asphalt and pitch, and the scent of burning human flesh. The air became foggy with terrible smoke, and as we sailed half-blind we began to hear the wails and cries of men.

We saw a natural harbour and moored our ship. Had we continued, barely able to see more than a few feet ahead, we might well have smashed into rocks. Setting foot on the island, there didn't appear to be any animals or even plants, there was bare rock everywhere.

Only after we had climbed a sheer cliff, did we see any plants, all big and ugly and full of thorns. As we hacked our way through, we saw that sword blades and metal traps protruded from the ground. During our trek, we came across three rivers; one of mud, one of blood and another of lava. The river of lava was impossible to cross. Peering into it, we could make out many fish swimming under the surface, some resembled coals, and others resembled flaming torches.

Walking alongside the fiery river, we came upon Timon of Athens. He was suspicious at first, but upon seeing Nauplius, he said that he would guide us. We were escorted to a part of the island where people, including kings, were being tormented with flames, as punishment for previous misdeeds. Those who endured the worst punishment, and whose voices we had earlier heard crying out, were those people who had told lies all their life, and written untrue histories. Among them I recognized Ctesias of Cnidos, and Heroditus. I was happy that such people were the ones who were punished, for I have never knowingly told a lie.

It was a horrific sight, and I could hardly endure the terrible screams, so we returned to the ship. Fortunately a change of wind had blown away the horrible fog, and after saying goodbye to Nauplius, we sailed away.

A few hours passed before the next island, the Island of Dreams, came into sight. It was somewhat vague in shape and position. As we approached, it would sometimes be nearer and sometimes further away, but before we gave up hope of ever reaching it, we suddenly found ourselves in a harbour, near some ivory gates.

Disembarking, we walked through the gates, then

between two springs and a river, and into the city mentioned only by Homer. Here there were trees that were not really trees at all, but tall poppies and mandragoras. Within them were bats, the only winged creatures to inhabit the island.

The wall that surrounded the city was rainbow-coloured, and there were not two city gates, as Homer says, but four. Two of these gates, one of iron and the other earthenware, were where nightmares exited, while the other two, including the one we passed through, faced the sea.

There was a temple in the city, to the right of the gate we entered, dedicated to the worship of the night, and to the left of the entrance was a palace where resides Sleep. There were two other temples in the heart of the town, one of falsehood and one of truth. It was said that Antiphon, the interpreter of dreams, also lived in this city.

Dreams made up the general population. Some dreams were tall and handsome, while others were squat and ugly. Some, it seemed to me were rich, while others resembled beggars.

We recognized many dreams, and many of them came to us and greeted us like old friends. They took us to their homes, put us to sleep, and entertained us as we slumbered. We stayed for a month, and during that time, one dream took me with him back to my homeland for one evening where I caught sight of my friends and family.

A great boom of thunder woke us all up, and we wondered if anything we had witnessed had really happened, and we once more set out to sea.

After three days we reached the island of Ogygia, and here I opened Odysseus's letter and read it:

Greetings dear Calypso,

I have not had the opportunity to tell you what happened to me after I left you, but now is my first chance. After I built the raft and left your island, I was shipwrecked. With Leucothea's help, I was able to journey home. When I arrived, I saw that my wife had many suitors, all of whom were living off her goodwill. I killed every one of them, but later on I was killed by Telegonus, my son by Circe. Now I live on the Island of the Blessed. I am sorry for having left you and your offer of immortality. If I ever get the chance, dear Calypso, I will leave this island and join you, and we might spend eternity together.

The letter also asked that Calypso entertain us, and we found her in a cave, close to the sea, much as Homer had described.

When Calypso read the letter, she wept. Eventually she dispelled her tears, and gave us a great feast. As we ate, she asked about Odysseus and about Penelope, and we gave her the answers that we thought she might wish to hear.

The next morning we left the island, only to be caught up in a storm that lasted two days. No sooner had the storm subsided however, than we were attacked by pirates. They sailed boats made of giant, hollowed-out melons, with reeds for masts and giant leaves for sails. As they attacked they hurled giant seeds at us, which were as hard as stones, and during hand-to-hand combat many of my crew were bludgeoned with them.

After an hour of deadlock, we saw men sailing ships made of giant nutshells. The melon-pirates left us as quickly as they had attacked and went off instead to fight the nut-people. We fled, knowing no good would come to us if we loitered, and I looked back now and again to see those on-board the nut-boats clearly had the upper hand and would eventually be victorious.

We attended to the wounded, and from that point kept a more vigilant lookout, lest we find ourselves caught off guard once more.

Our vigilance paid off, for as we passed a desert island, we saw twenty men riding dolphins as though they were horses. The dolphins leapt and dived and neighed, and the men, who we soon discovered were also pirates, never lost their balance. When they were only yards away, they bombarded us with dry cuttle-fish and crabs' eyes. We threw spears and arrows back at them, and they were soon beaten, and they fled back to their island where they tended to the wounded.

Our next encounter took place at around midnight when, in the darkness, we ran aground, and found we had become stranded on a giant bird's nest, made not of twigs but of trees. The nest was floating and indeed moving, pulled by the currents, and in the middle of the nest a giant bird was sitting on her eggs. She began to cry out and beat her wings, and the wind they created almost sunk our ship. She flew up and out of sight, and while she was gone, we cut open some of the eggs with our axes. Inside were featherless chicks, larger than twenty vultures, and we took one of them back to the ship. After moving some tree branches to free our ship, we were able to set sail.

We had travelled ten leagues or so, when the chick we had captured began to suddenly sprout feathers. What was even more amazing was that Scintharus, who was completely bald, now had a thick head of hair. More astounding still was the mast which, suddenly grew branches, then leaves and figs.

We prayed to the gods, for we were very disturbed by these strange and sudden occurrences. Ahead, we saw a forest of pine trees and cypresses, and indeed this forest seemed to run the length of the horizon in front of us. But all was not as it seemed. As we came closer, we saw that this was not a densely wooded island, but rootless trees, upright and floating.

As we could not go round, or thought it would take too long to do so, we made a rope, climbed the trees and pulled the ship up. The trees were so closely packed that they easily held us and our vessel. We clambered aboard, spread our canvas and, with a good wind behind us, we sailed across the treetops as easily as crossing the ocean.

Reaching the other side of the strange wood, we let the boat down once more, and continued our journey through clear waters.

Our next obstacle was something quite different; the ocean had a great crack running the length of it, as though made by some great earthquake. We were blown right to the edge, where I looked down to see a sheer drop of at least a thousand furlongs. The water did not tumble down however, instead it remained where it was. To our right, at no great distance, was a river, bridging the crack. We rowed away from the edge, and with some effort we crossed the watery bridge.

The sea on the other side was quite calm, and we reached a small island where we saw people who resembled the great Minotaur. They were a savage race. We were out of food and water, and having taken water from a river, we went in search of food. But we had not gone far when we heard a bellow. At first we thought we had come across cattle, but then we were attacked by these bull-men. Three of my crew were captured and the rest of us were chased back to our ship. We did not have to talk for long before agreeing to go back and avenge our friends. We armed ourselves, and went back, attacking the bull-men as they feasted on our companions.

We killed fifty of them and took two back to our ship as prisoners. We still had no food and some of the hungry crew suggested we eat our enemy. But I had other ideas, and we clasped the bull-men in irons and waited until a delegation of bull-men approached us. In return for the two captives we were given cheeses, fish, onions, and four does, each of which had only three legs – two hind legs and fused forelegs.

We did not wait any more time than necessary before once more setting out to sea. We soon saw fish and birds and other signs that we were approaching land, and travelling a little further we saw beings that were both sailors and ships. They lay on their backs, on the water, and they tied sails to a certain part of their anatomy which they used as masts. Others, sat on corks and were pulled along by dolphins. These strange people neither attacked nor fled from us, but wondered at our boat with quizzical looks.

As dusk came, we anchored our ship by a small island, inhabited by women, or so we thought. They were all young and wore tunics that swept the ground, and to our surprise they all spoke perfect Greek. They also made us feel most welcome, and embraced every one of us.

Each woman escorted one man back to their home and made him her guest. I was invited back by a most beautiful young woman, but I had my misgivings and declined her invitation. As my companions disappeared, I wandered round and saw human bones and skulls. I was tempted to shout aloud and call my crew back, but instead I grabbed my mallow, and prayed to it.

I returned to the spot where I had declined the young woman's invitation and saw that she was still there, waiting. I let her escort me back to her home, and it was as we entered that I glimpsed not her feet, but hooves. Startled I made a few more surreptitious glances and saw that her legs were those of an ass.

I drew my sword, caught her and held the blade against her neck. I asked her who she was and what her people intended to do with my men.

"We are women of the sea," she said. "When we have intoxicated your men, we will kill them and eat them."

I tied her up and ran outside where I called for my companions. I told them the story and showed them the bones, but when I took them to the woman I had tied up, she had turned to a pool of water. I took my sword and plunged it into the water, which quickly turned crimson.

We fled to the boat and sailed away in the darkness. By dawn, we saw land on the horizon, and none of us doubted that this was the continent that Rhadamanthus had told us about; the continent on the other side of the world. We made an offering to the gods, and discussed whether or not our expedition should end here. Some argued that we had been fortunate enough to get this far, and that now was the time to go home. Others said we should explore the continent's interior.

But the elements made the decision for us – a storm like none we had encountered before whipped up in a matter of minutes and our ship was thrown towards the land and smashed upon rocks. We all swam towards the beach, and to an uncertain future.

So now I have told you of our trip to the Moon, our adventure inside the great whale, our time with the heroes, and the host of strange islands we visited, but what happened in this other world will be revealed to you in the next book.

Icaro-Menippus

Lucian of Samosata

Introduction

Lucian of Samosata (125–c.180) was a Greek satirist of Syrian or Assyrian extraction, and is perhaps best-known for his story *True History*. *Icaro-Menippus* is a satirical play with Greek philosophers being the focus of Lucian's ridicule. The play contains only two characters: Menippus, and an unnamed friend. Mennipus tells his companion how he used bird wings to fly into space, visiting the Moon and the Greek gods during his travels. Whether or not Mennipus's story is true is left for the audience to decide.

Characters in the Play

Menippus
An Unnamed Friend

Icaro-Menippus

Lucian of Samosata

[A friend overhears Menippus talking to himself, and approaches him.]

MENIPPUS (muttering): Now let me think. The distance from the Earth to the Moon is around three hundred and forty miles. And then to the Sun, that must be another fifteen hundred miles. And from there to Heaven and to Jupiter's palace, well, by my reckoning that's about the distance a swift eagle might cover in a day.

FRIEND: What are you whispering, Menippus? I've been following you these last few minutes, listening as you talk to yourself in a most abstracted manner, about the Moon and the stars and the Sun, and the distances between them.

MENNIPUS: Don't be too amazed if my words sound strange and startling. I am simply calculating the distance I travelled on my latest journey.

FRIEND: I see. You've been using the night sky to help you find your bearings, just as the Phoenicians do.

MENIPPUS: You are wrong my friend. I haven't used the Moon and the Heavens to guide me – I have just returned from travelling among the stars themselves.

FRIEND: You mean you have had a dream – and a long dream at that if you travelled such vast distances.

MENIPPUS: It was no dream. I have just returned from Jupiter!

FRIEND: What? You mean you have literally descended from the Heavens?

MENIPPUS: That is exactly what happened. I have only just returned from Jupiter, where I heard and saw the strangest things. I see you doubt me, but no matter, it makes my trip even more satisfying when I think it is beyond the belief of others.

FRIEND: How could a man as humble as myself not believe the words of the divine Menippus? How could I doubt the word of someone, who has flown above the clouds, and who Homer might call an 'inhabitant of Heaven'? But tell me how you managed to reach such lofty heights. Where did you find a ladder big enough for you to climb so high – or were you snatched up by a giant eagle, and whisked off into the Heavens?

MENIPPUS: I'm not surprised you see my story as a joke, given all I have said, but my story is no fable, I assure you. I needed no ladder, or an eagle, for I had wings of my own.

FRIEND: Why this is more amazing than the tale of Daedalus and Icarus! Did you turn into a hawk or some other bird when we were not looking?

MENIPPUS: Well, for all your scoffing, you are quite close to the truth. I did copy Daedalus's idea of using wings to fly.

FRIEND: Well if you tried that idea then you're a fool. Did you want the wax that held your feathers in place to melt, so that you might plunge into the sea, and have it named after you just as happened to Icarus? I can imagine it now – The Menippean Sea.

MENIPPUS: I had no such intention. I did not use wax because I didn't want to plunge from the sky like Icarus.

FRIEND: Then what did you use?

MENIPPUS: I caught a powerful eagle and a large vulture, and then I cut off their wings for my own use. If you have the time I will happily tell you, from beginning to end, of my flight into the Heavens.

FRIEND: Please do. I would love to know what happened. I feel like the suspense – suspended by the ears that is – is all too much.

MENIPPUS: Listen then – I would never leave a friend who has been suspended by his ears.

I had thought much about human affairs like wealth and power, law and politics and so on, and I came to the conclusion that such things were trivial and near-worthless, not least compared with the majesty of the universe. I was excited to meditate on things that to me were new and profound: How had the universe come into being? Who had made it? Had there been a beginning – and would there be an end?

But the more I investigated, the more confused I became. I looked up at the stars, seemingly scattered at random across the sky, I looked at the Sun and wondered what it was made of, and I looked at the Moon, which appeared to me to be the most magnificent thing in the sky, and I wondered why on some nights it was full and on others it was not. I puzzled over the descent of rain and hail and snow, and I wanted to know about thunder and lightning. All of these things swirled in my mind and I longed to know their nature.

I thought that to get some answers I would be best off consulting the philosophers. I was sure they could put my mind at rest. So I selected the best of them, judging their wisdom by their complexion, their poses, and the length of their beards. After choosing from these many men with their lofty thoughts and even loftier words, I placed myself in their hands. And after happily taking a tidy some of money, and receiving my guarantee that they would receive yet more money after my training, they began to instruct me.

I had hoped that I would become a man of wisdom, and a great orator on many profound subjects. But far from dispelling my ignorance, they instead managed to confuse me even more, with their talk of atoms and voids, beginnings and ends, matter and form, and goodness knows what else. And worst of all, they couldn't even agree with one another, and each of them expected me to believe him, and subscribe to his beliefs.

FRIEND: How funny that such wise men should disagree so vehemently, holding so many opinions on the same things.

MENIPPUS: You'll find it funnier still when I tell you about their pretentious drivel. These philosophers, who are no taller than ourselves yet walk about with self-satisfied grandeur, are neither wiser nor sharper-sighted than the rest of us, and yet they go about saying how they can measure the circumference of the Sun, work out the shape and size of stars and even walk upon the Moon. All these lofty claims, from men who could not say how many miles it is from Athens to Megara. They even claim to be able to calculate the distance from the Moon to the Sun, how high the atmosphere is and the depth of the sea. I have seen them scribbling down numbers, and drawing squares and triangles and circles, and then suddenly they cry that they have calculated the volume of Heaven itself.

They happily speak without the slightest self-doubt. They swear that the Sun is a molten mass of liquid fire, that the Moon is inhabited, that the stars drink water, and that the Sun draws vapour from the sea be means of a bucket and rope, before shedding the load across the world.

They disagree with each other on so many points. Some believe that the world had no beginning and can have no end, some say the world, and indeed the universe, had a Creator, and talk as though they know everything about Him. But they will not say where he came from, nor where he resides, nor how the ideas of time and space could have existed before the universe began.

FRIEND: They really do sound like a bunch of verbal conjurers.

MENIPPUS: I wish I could tell you more about their arguments over ideal and incorporeal substances, and over things finite and infinite. On the latter point there is much disagreement. Some philosophers believe everything has boundaries, others say there are no limits. Some say there is but one world, while others say there are many. There is even one man who claims that war is the father of the universe.

When it comes to divinity they are even more divided. Some say god is a number, while others swear by dogs and geese and trees. Some say there is only one god – an idea I find almost too depressing to contemplate. Others furnish their theories with a liberal sprinkling of gods, giving them tasks to undertake, and also rank them according to divinity. Some assumed the gods were entities that neither had substance nor shape. Others believed they had bodies, like most living creatures. There was disagreement over whether or not gods intervened in human affairs. Some philosophers claimed the gods intervened at regular intervals, while their philosopher-opponents claimed that the gods resided in the background, like men who had retired from civic duty.

Some philosophers went further still and claimed that there were no gods at all. They asserted that the world drifts without any guide or master.

I listened intently to every philosopher and, to begin with at least, I did not dare contradict any of those men with their long words and longer beards. But as they contradicted one another I became confused. Whenever I thought that one of them had a valid point and I began to believe that they had struck upon an unassailable truth, doubts would creep into my mind.

But during my distress, and perhaps as a result of it, I decided that rather than use theory and counter theory to discover truths about the universe, why not travel there and see the answer for myself? So it was that I decided to escape these men of words, and to fashion myself some wings and fly to the Heavens. Indeed I was heartened when picking up a copy of Aesop's Fables, and read that beetles, eagles and even camels had succeeded in reaching the Heavens.

Obviously I could not sprout wings of my own, so I decided to use those of an eagle and a vulture – wings that were powerful enough to lift a man from the ground, of course. I caught an eagle, and a vulture, and I amputated the eagle's right wing and the vulture's left wing. I fastened them to my arms with loops of material, and near the wing tips were two more loops for my hands to hold.

Then I was ready to begin my experiments. To begin with I simply jumped up and down and flapped my wings. Then I began to imitate geese, the way they spread out their wings and run across the ground and take off. To begin with I simply skimmed the ground, but then I became bold and ventured to the top of the Acropolis. Steeling myself, I leapt, and found myself not falling but flying downwards into the theatre. Landing safely, I found almost all my fear had disappeared. Starting from Hymettus I flew to Geranea. From there I flew on to the top of the tower at Corinth, and then I travelled over Pholoe, and then from Erymanthus to Taygetus.

But this was merely a chicken's flight compared with my ultimate aim. Now my training was complete, and my arms were powerfully strong. I took provisions with me and soared up to the top of Mount Olympus.

The Heavens were above me and the world far below me, and from here I soared further into the sky. Looking down as I flew made me feel quite giddy at first, but this soon wore off. I looked ahead and set my course for the Moon.

I had not planned to land on the Moon, and soon even the clouds were far behind me, but by this point I was tiring, especially in the vulture wing. So as soon as I reached the Moon I decided to land.

I sat myself down and, with my bird's-eye view, I looked back upon the Earth. So, like Homer's Jupiter, I was able to survey the Thracian horsemen, the Mycians, and the people of India, Persia and Greece. All of whom I observed with great delight.

FRIEND: Tell me everything you can about your travels, and don't omit a single detail. Recount, if you would, all you saw and heard. I would love to know the shape of the Earth, and how it appeared to someone who stood upon the Moon, observing it.

MENIPPUS: I will tell you all you desire. But first you will have to travel, in your imagination, to the Moon, with my words for guidance. Then turn to face the Earth. When I was there and looked down upon the Earth, it appeared to me to be far smaller than the Moon. At first I could not make out the great mountains of the Earth, or the vast seas, until I spotted the colossus of Rhodes, and the tower of Pharus. Indeed without spotting these great monuments, it would have been impossible to recognise our world.

But my eyes soon began to focus and make sense of what they saw, and when the light from the Sun grew a little stronger and began to glint off the ocean waves, I was able to make out a great deal. I could see nations and cities and the whole of the human race. I saw men waging war, ploughing fields and sailing the seas, and I saw women, animals and, in short, I beheld every creature that roamed upon the Earth.

FRIEND: That really is a most unconvincing and contradictory story Menippus. You said that the Earth was tiny in size, far smaller than the Moon. You said that had it not been for the colossus of Rhodes you wouldn't have seen it at all. Then, you contradict yourself, and talk of being able to make out men and women and animals. Had I let you talk further, no doubt you would have told me how you observed, from that great distance, a nest of fleas.

MENIPPUS: Of course – thank you for reminding me! I forgot to mention that at first I had been able to make out the Earth but as it was so far away, I could not pick out any particular details on its surface. I was horribly frustrated by my situation and felt I might burst into tears, but before I was swallowed whole by misery who should turn up but the physicist Empedocles. He looked as black as coal, covered in ashes, and scorched as though he'd just stepped out of an oven. I must admit to having been terrified upon seeing this strange figure, thinking he was some sort of Moon Creature.

"Do not be afraid," he reassured me. "I am no demon, but a man like yourself. Friend, I am Empedocles, the physicist. You may know the tale of how I climbed to the summit Mount Etna, and threw myself into its volcanic crater. But I did not die, instead the billowing smoke lifted me high into the Heavens and deposited me here. Now I live on the Moon, feeding on dew, and spending most of my days philosophizing. I can see you are distressed, and I am here to help you fulfil your wish to see everything on Earth."

"Thank you Empedocles," I said. "When I return to Greece, I will burn offerings to you, and will send them up my chimney once every month."

"There is no need," said Empedocles. "I am not helping you so that I might be rewarded. I was saddened to see your distress, so decided to help. Now what do you think might help you see in great detail all that goes on, amongst the humans of Earth?"

"I have no idea," I said. "It all seems so hazy. It is as though my eyes are straining to see through mist, and unless you can get rid of this blurred vision I doubt I'll be able to see anything."

"You don't need me to improve your sight," said Empedocles. "You have brought the necessary piece of equipment with you."

"Really?" I said, rather startled.

"Of course," he replied. "It is your eagle's wing, which you wear on your right arm."

"But how does that help?" I asked. "What has an eagle's wing to do with improving my eyesight?"

"A lot," he replied. "As you may know, the eagle has the best eyesight of any living creature. This bird is the only one that can stare at the Sun without blinking."

"So I have heard," I said. "But I do not have the eyes of an eagle. Perhaps I should have not only taken the eagle's wing, but his eyes also and replaced mine with them."

"You may still acquire one eagle eye," said Empedocles.

I looked at him, puzzled.

He continued: "You must beat your eagle wing up and down, while keeping the vulture wing absolutely still. As you do this, your right eye will gain in strength, until you are able to see all you wish to on the world below. Your left eye however, being on the side of the vulture wing will always remain inferior, and there is nothing that can be done about this."

"I am happy enough to have such brilliance of vision in just one eye," I said. "I do not need it in both. Indeed I have seen carpenters and artists occasionally making use of just one eye rather than two, and if it is good enough for them, it is good enough for me."

I began at once to flap my eagle wing and, knowing his work was done, Empedocles turned into smoke, then faded and disappeared.

FRIEND: That really is astounding.

MENIPPUS: Indeed, and there were still more amazing things to come. So I continued to beat my wing, and as I did so the mist lifted from before my eyes and I was able to see the world with the sharpness of an eagle.

Looking down on the Earth, I could see cities and men and all that took place. Strangely, I was able to see not only what took place in the open but what happened inside people's homes. I saw Lysimachus plotting to execute his eldest son, Agathocles; Antiochus conspiring with his mother-in-law; Alexander the Thessalian being killed by his wife; Attalus being poisoned by his son; Arsaces murdering his mistress; the eunuch Arbaces killing Arsaces; guards dragging Spatinus the Mede from the banquet by his heels and then struck over the head with a golden cup.

In the palaces of Scythia and Lybia and Thrace I saw nothing but murder, adultery, treason, robbery, conspiracies, suspicion and people betrayed by their so-called friends. So this was the life lead by royalty and nobility, but in the private houses there was still more to see. I saw Hermodorus the Epicurean perjuring himself for a thousand dracmas; Agathocles the Stoic trying to extract fees from one of his pupils;

The orator, Clinias, stealing a phial from the temple of Asclepius, and I saw Herophilus the Cynic visiting a brothel.

And then there was the rest of the population, robbers, burglars, fraudsters and others who put on a fine spectacle for me.

FRIEND: What entertainment! I wish I'd been there with you to witness it all. But please, tell me more.

MENIPPUS: I'm afraid I saw too much to recount to you here. Indeed so much went on even my eagle eye could not take it all in. There were feasts and marriages, arguments and burials. The Getae were at war, there were Scythians travelling in their caravans, the Egyptians were ploughing their fields, the Cilicians were robbing and plundering, the Phoenicians were flogging their wares, the Spartans were flogging one another, and the Athenians – a litigious lot – were forever taking one another to court.

All this was happening simultaneously, you must understand, and it was all rather confusing. It was as though a choir had been told not to sing harmoniously, but to sing their own songs, and to ensure that they were heard above the rest. I'm sure you can imagine what a deafening cacophony it would be.

FRIEND: It must have been the most ridiculous and confusing sight.

MENIPPUS: Alas, it was. All those Earthly performers putting on their confused spectacle, and showing that the life of man is just that – a confused spectacle. Their voices are discordant, their movements are not synchronous, the set is not agreed upon, and so it goes on, until the director dismisses every one of them from the stage, telling them they are no longer wanted. Then they are all silent, and no longer shout over one another in this cacophonous chorus. This theatre is wide and diverse, where there is plenty to ridicule and laugh about.

Those who entertained me the most however, were those who argued and fought over the boundaries of their tiny territories, or thought themselves high and mighty because they worked on the plains of Sicyon, or those who prided themselves on holding the border between Marathon and Oenoe, or those who fancied themselves because they owned a thousand acres in Acharnae.

As I gazed down at Greece, it appeared so small that it might have fitted in the palm of my hand. And Athens, well, it was truly minute. I realized that these pompous men were priding themselves over the tiniest pieces of land. The greatest landowner of them all appeared to be lord of nothing more than an atom.

I glanced towards the Peloponnese, and towards Cynuria, where I saw that for the tiniest fragment of land, no bigger than a lentil, an astonishing number of Spartans and Argives were slaughtered.

I also saw a man who thought far too much of himself because he owned eight gold rings and four gold cups – I could help but laugh at the fellow! Even Pangaeus, with all its mines, seemed no larger than a grain of millet.

FRIEND: What a sight that must have been. I would dearly love to know how large the towns and their residents seemed to you.

MENIPPUS: I'm sure you've seen ants scurrying about, sometimes alone and sometimes in great numbers busying themselves in their own little city. One might be rolling something, another pushing a bean or a grain of wheat. Even on their tiny scale, I have no doubt that they have their own architects, politicians, musicians, philosophers and the like. And when I looked down, to see men and their cities, they reminded me of ants and their ant-hills. If you think my comparison too unfair, then you would do well to recollect the Thessalian tales, and you will find that the Myrmidons – ants that had turned into men – were the most war-like of people.

When I had had my fill of observing all of humanity on this tiny planet, and meditating on the insignificance of human affairs, I turned my back, started to jog and then run, and as I pick up speed my feet left the ground. But before I could begin my flight towards the land of the Gods, the Moon in her soft, feminine voice cried out to me:

"Menippus!"

I landed back on the ground.

"Menippus," she said again, "please take with you something of mine to Jupiter. If you do, I promise that you shall prosper from your journey."

"I would gladly carry something for you," I replied. "So long as I am strong enough to take it with me."

"It weighs nothing at all," said the Moon. "It is a

message that I wish you to take; a petition addressed to Jupiter himself. I have become so very tired by the philosophers of your world – I am almost at my wit's end. They seem to have nothing better to do than talk about me, as though I have no feelings. Just how big am I? they ask. Who am I? Why am I sometimes full, sometimes half-full and sometimes vanish altogether? Am I merely a mirror hanging over the sea? Am I inhabited? I'm so tired of their endless speculations and conjectures. And just when I thought they couldn't get any worse, they began to suggest the light that I radiate is not my own, but stolen from my own brother, the Sun. I can't believe they would suggest such a thing, and try to turn us against one another. It was bad enough when they said he was a red-hot stone, but now they've really gone too far.

"These philosophers, with their long beards and grave countenances, who act so rationally during the day, would be surprised to know that I see exactly what they get up to at night. But I say nothing of their adultery or thieving or any other shameful pursuit. I have never even considered making these facts known to the wider public, instead, when I see their vile ways, I wrap myself in a thick cloud. I don't want to watch these dirty old creatures and their disgusting habits.

"But these fiends, guilty of every vice, go on abusing me and sullying my reputation. It has upset me so greatly, that I have often considered flying away so that I might never see or hear another philosopher again.

"Please, tell Jupiter all that I have said, and that if nothing is done I will leave, never to return. I want him to destroy all physicists, silence the logicians and burn the Academy down, so that I might finally have the rest which these so-called wise men perpetually deny me."

"I will pass your message on," I promised, and I flew into the air, and away from the Moon, until she was quite small, and the Earth was hidden behind her.

With the Sun on my right hand side, I flew for three days through the stars, where no man had travelled before, until I finally reached my destination – the entrance to Heaven. My first thought was to fly straight in. The eagle was well known to Jupiter, and now being half an eagle, I thought I might enter without raising any suspicion. But it then occurred to me that my vulture wing might betray me. So instead I walked up to the door and knocked.

Mercury answered the door, and after I had told him my name, he went to inform Jupiter. Upon Mercury's return, he asked me to step in, and I did so, trembling with apprehension.

I soon saw, right in front of me, the gods, sitting together, looking at me with suspicion and more than a little fear. I imagined that they were worried that I might be the first of an army of winged mortals on their way to the land of the gods.

Jupiter looked straight at me with a Titanic and penetrating stare.

"Who are you?" he boomed. "From where have you come? From whom are you descended?"

Such was the thunder of his voice, I thought I might die from fright. But I somehow remained standing, though at first I was unable to speak, such was my condition. I was able to compose myself, and then I recounted my whole tale: how I had been fascinated by the Heavens and wanted to know all about them; how I had visited the philosophers, only to hear them contradict one another and ultimately leave me none the wiser; how I had decided to seek the answers for myself and made wings and flown from Earth to Heaven.

I told him too of my visit to the Moon, and told him of her woes, just as she had asked. When Jupiter was told this, his hard expression softened, and then he gave me a large smile.

"Who are Otus and Ephialtes in comparison with Menippus?" said Jupiter. "This mortal man who stands before us has flown up to Heaven. Mennipus, you may stay here the evening as our guest, and tomorrow we will discuss matters of business, and then you may return to Earth."

When he had finished speaking, he stood up and, beckoning me, took me on a journey to a part of Heaven where people's prayers and petitions could be heard. As we walked he asked me a great many questions: How much wheat is there presently in Greece? Had the previous winter been a harsh one? Did our vegetables need more rain? Were any of Phidias's family still alive? Why had Athenians stopped making their sacrifices to the gods? Were they going to continue building the Olympian temple again? Had the robbers that had plundered the temple at Dodona been caught?

I was fortunate to be able to answer all his questions, to his apparent satisfaction, and then he asked another:

"Pray tell me, Menippus – what do people really think about me?"

"Why," I replied, "they think of you just as they should – they look upon the king of gods with the greatest respect and veneration."

"Come now," said Jupiter, "I know that's not true. But long ago I was well respected, when I healed the sick, answered their prayers, and did almost everything that was asked of me.

"Back then Dodona and Pisa were two of the finest places on Earth, and I was unable to see them through all the smoke that came from their sacrifices. Now though it's all changed: Apollo has set up his oracle at Delphi; Aesculapius practices as a healer at Pergamus; temples have been erected to Bendis at Thrace, to Anubis in Egypt, and to Diana at Ephesus. Now people flock to these places instead, and devote themselves to other gods. If they make some sacrificial offering to me every few years at Mount Olympus, people think they're being more than generous.

"It really does seem as though I'm surplus to requirements these days. Now people are about as interested in my altars as they are in Plato's laws, or even Chrysippus's syllogisms."

So we walked on, until we reached the part of Heaven where people's prayers and petitions could be heard. Here there was a row of shafts, each with a lid over the top, and next to each one was a gold chair.

Jupiter seated himself, and opened the first lid. I could hear a babble of voices, and I knelt by the side of the hole, trying to discern what was being said. I was able to snatch a few wishes:

"Oh, Jupiter! Make me the ruler of a large and wealthy empire!"

"Dear gods, let my vegetables flourish!"

"Jupiter – please kill my father!"

"Jupiter – let my wife die, so that I might inherit her property!"

"I beg of you – do not let them find out about my treacherous plans against my brother!"

"Let me be victorious in my impending trial."

"Jupiter, let me be crowned at Olympia."

I heard these and more. One wish was from a sailor who desired a north wind, while another sailor prayed for a south wind. I heard one farmer wish for more Sunlight and another wish for rain.

Jupiter listened patiently, and after careful consideration he granted what he considered to be righteous prayers to come up the shaft and into Heaven. Then he blew all those prayers he considered unworthy back down, so that they would not pollute Heaven.

I remember one case where Jupiter was puzzled. Two men asked for contrary wishes to be granted, much like the two who had desired opposing winds, and to make things even more difficult, they had offered Jupiter the same sacrifice as a token. Jupiter did not know who to favour, and he became a brilliant academic, whose mind was able to hold these opposite wishes in perfect equilibrium, just like Pyrrho.

When he had finally dispensed with the prayers, he passed onto the next seat and lifted the lid of another shaft. Here he took on board vows being made and oaths being sworn.

Next he destroyed Hermodorus the Epicurean, who had been found guilty of perjury. On the following seat, Jupiter dealt with auguries, prophets and sooth sayers. After that, hc sat by the shaft where the smoke of the sacrificed dead wafted up and into Heaven, and where those sacrificed told Jupiter the names of those who had sacrificed them.

Once he had heard all the names, he gave orders to the elements:

"Let there be rain in Scythia today, thunder and lightning across the North of Africa, and snow in Greece. The North Wind shall blow in Lydia while the South Wind shall rest today. I want a storm to be raised in the Adriatic, and hail to be cast over Cappadocia."

At last his work in this strange place was done and the lids were closed once more. We retired from this part of Heaven and feasted with the other gods. Mercury guided me to me seat, and I found myself in the company of lesser-gods Pan, the Corybantes, Attis, and Sabazius.

I was handed some bread by Ceres, and Baccus poured me plenty of wine. Hercules dished out the meat, Venus gave out myrtle, and Neptune doled out sea food. While my dining companions were occupied in eating or conversation, good-natured Ganymede slipped me a little nectar and ambrosia without anyone noticing. The Gods, as Homer says (and presumably he has gained such knowledge by visiting Heaven as I have) never feast on bread nor wine, but instead eat ambrosia and drink nectar. Their favourite indulgence however is neither of these, for the gods love nothing more than to inhale the fumes that rise up from victims, and smell the blood of those sacrificed on altars.

During the meal we were treated to many fine performances: Apollo played his harp, Silenus danced, and the Muses sang many songs for us, including Pindar's first ode. After we had eaten and had been greatly entertained, we all slept. Or, I should say, the gods all slept, but my mind was too restless, frothing with a myriad of thoughts. How was it, I wondered, that Apollo in his many years had never grown a beard? With the Sun present, how was it that I could see the night sky?

Eventually I was able to slide into a brief slumber, and early in the morning Jupiter arose and woke the rest of us up. He gathered the gods together into an assembly and addressed them:

"I am addressing you this morning," he began. "because of the stranger who came here yesterday and is with us still. I have wanted, for some time, to discuss the matter of the philosophers, and now that the Moon has petitioned us, it is time we did something about this matter. There is a group that has, in recent times, come about; a group of the laziest, most quarrelsome, vain, foolish, greedy, rude, pompous men to have walked upon the Earth. They have split into many groups who each wrap themselves in an impenetrable shroud of words, and call themselves Stoics, Epicureans, Peripatetics, and too many other names to count. They call themselves virtuous, and with their eyebrows and flowing beards they put on a great appearance of morality to hide their immoral behaviour. It is a performance, worthy of any actor who, if you pulled off his mask and robe, would be seen for what he is – a weedy man hired to appear for a few drachmas.

"These philosophers happily go around despising everyone, they spread lies about the gods, and gather together gullible young men and fill their minds with worthless information. These young disciples are told by their masters to scorn riches and pleasures, and to embrace fortitude and temperance. These same masters who, when they are alone, indulge in every form of debauchery. But their worst offence is that they do nothing and help no one. They contribute no good to society, they merely sneer at ordinary folk, continually finding fault in the words and actions of people in their community.

"If someone were to ask a philosopher, 'What useful role do you play in society?' he, if he had the ability to speak fairly and truthfully, would reply, 'It is beneath my dignity to be a farmer or sailor or soldier, or work in trade. But I do have a loud voice and a dirty body, I scrub myself in cold water, and go barefoot all winter and then, like Momus, I find fault with others. If a wealthy man purchases something expensive, I abuse him. If a friend is ill, and needs help and care, I take no notice of them.'

"This then is the kind of man we are dealing with. And of all these philosophers, the Epicureans are the worst. They say the gods take no interest in human affairs, and have no effect on the course of human lives. If these Epicureans spread their beliefs, and people think that we do nothing for them, then they will no longer make sacrifices, and we will starve. As to the Moon's complaints, you heard all this from the stranger yesterday.

"Now you must decide among yourselves what is to be done with these philosophers, both for the benefit of ourselves and the happiness of mankind."

Jupiter had barely finished speaking, when the gods cried out: "Blast them with thunder and lightning! Burn them all! Throw them all the way down to Tartarus, and to the giants!"

Jupiter raised his hand and asked for silence. "Your will shall be done," his voice boomed. "The philosophers shall be destroyed along with their philosophy – but not just yet. As you are all aware, I have declared a truce for the next four months, but when Spring comes, and the truce is over, I shall fire lightning bolts at them and give them the punishment they deserve."

Then, as soon as the counsel began to break up, my wings were removed, and I was carried by Mercury back down to Earth.

So now my friend you have heard my story, and know all about Heaven. But I really must be off to the Poecile, and tell my good news to the philosophers.

Urashima Taro

Introduction

Urashima Taro is the earliest known time-travel tale. This story was written by an unknown Japanese author and dates from around the eighth century. It tells of a fisherman who saves a turtle from being tormented by children, and who is rewarded with a trip beneath the sea to the palace of a dragon god. He stays for just three days, but when he returns to his homeland he finds himself transported three hundred years into the future.

Urashima Taro

Many years ago on the south coast of Japan there lived a young fisherman called Urashima Taro. He was well-liked by all the people in his village, and when he wasn't fishing, he spent his days caring for his sickly mother. He was also very brave, and would just as likely go out to the sea in a storm as on a calm day, and the locals could not say if he was fearless or foolhardy.

One day, while walking along the sea shore, Urashima Taro saw a knot of children throwing stones at something and laughing. As he approached the children, he saw that they were tormenting a small female turtle. He ran at the youngsters and they scattered before he could catch any of them.

Urashima Taro picked up the turtle and, seeing its shell had protected it against any serious injury, placed it back in the sea.

Day after day for a whole year he continued to fish in all weathers, despite his mother's concern that one day he might never return. One evening, during a particularly fierce storm, his boat was buffeted and blown further and further out to sea. Rain lashed him, and thunder and lightning boomed and flashed all about the boat.

Try as he might, Urashima Taro could not control his boat as the wind and waves did their best to throw him towards a lonely outcrop of black rocks. He was tossed off the boat just as it smashed into the rocks, and he watched as his beloved vessel was smashed to pieces and dragged beneath the waves.

Urashima Taro swam towards the outcrop and clung on to one of the rocks, watching as huge waves boomed and burst all about him. He clung on for what felt like an eternity, but before his weakening arms gave out, he saw something rise from beneath the water's surface.

A giant turtle appeared.

"Urashima Taro," she said, "a year ago you saved my life. "Now climb on my back and let me save yours."

Urashima Taro did not wait, and in a moment he had clambered onto the turtle's back.

"I cannot take you home right now," said the turtle, "the weather is too bad. I will have to take you back to my home in the Palace of the Dragon God."

Urashima Taro barely had time to grab underneath the turtle's shell and hold tight before they began to plunge down into the depths of the ocean. At first he could not breath, and he began to panic. He felt a flicker of pain on either side of his throat, and when he touched his neck, he could feel gills. Now he was able to breath the water as though it was air.

Soon they had swum fathoms down and were on the ocean floor. They were outside a magnificent coral palace, which Urashimo Taro could see was inlaid with gold and silver and colourful gems.

Stepping inside, accompanied by the great turtle, Urashima Taro was met by a beautiful and refined young woman. She wore a shimmering blue dress and a necklace of coloured shells. The turtle introduced them to one another.

"Princess Otohime, this is Urashima Taro – the young man who rescued me from those cruel children."

"You did us all a great service, Urashima Taro," said the Princess.

Urashima Taro was entranced by the Princess's beauty, and she too seemed smitten by the visitor.

"Please do stay with us a while," she said. "I hope our hospitality will go some way towards thanking you for rescuing my turtle."

Urashima Taro was invited to dine, and as he sat down he watched fascinated as fish darted past him.

"How do you find the palace?" said the Princess.

"It is a most beautiful place," Urashima Taro replied.

"Do you think me beautiful?" the Princess asked.

"You are the prettiest woman I have ever seen," he replied. "You are every bit as pretty as the palace you live in."

Urashima Taro had hoped to see the Dragon God during his stay, but that was not to be, and after three days, he said to the Princess: "My love, I must return to my world and see my mother."

"Please do not go," said Princess Otohime. "Stay in my world, where you can become my husband and Prince of this world, and stay young forever."

Urashima Taro shook his head. "My mother is ill, and I fear she only has days to live. I must go back and see her. Love, do not look at me with those sad eyes. I will return the moment I am able."

"If you go, you will never come back," said the Princess.

"Have faith in me, Otohime. When I am ready to return I will call out for your turtle, and she will bring me back."

"I cannot stop you, Urishima Taro, but if you go, you must take this box with you." Princess Otohime handed him a box of coral and jade. "Keep it with you at all times, but promise me you will never open it. Do this and my turtle will meet you on the shore and bring you back."

"I promise," he said.

The Princess bade him farewell.

"Goodbye Princess," he replied, and he climbed on the turtle's back.

Urashima Taro was taken along the sea bed, its gradient rising very slowly. After a few hours of travelling, the sea became so shallow that Urashima Taro was able to jump off the turtle and wade ashore.

Reaching the beach, Urashima Taro stared, puzzled. The shoreline still looked the same – yet something had changed.

The houses are different, he realized.

All the houses that had been there as long as he could remember were gone. Now there were different buildings. Urashima Taro walked to his village. Here too the houses had changed, and only a few that he knew still stood, looking far shabbier than he remembered.

He had known almost every person in his village too, but now every face that looked at him was that of a stranger.

Ahead, he saw his old home, looking very neglected, and he knocked on the door with some trepidation.

An unfamiliar old woman answered.

"Yes?"

Urashima Taro asked if his mother still lived there.

"I've lived here almost eighty years, and my mother and grandmother lived here before me," she replied. "I think you must be mistaken young man."

No person in the village had heard of his mother or any of his friends, and he was directed to a wise old man who might be able to help. The old man listened to Urashima Taro's tale, then thought a moment, as if trying to recall some distant memory.

At last he nodded his head. "Come with me," he said and rose unsteadily to his feet.

He led Urashima Taro out of the village and up a hill towards the cemetery. The area it covered seemed greater than Urashima Taro remembered.

"Check the headstones," said the old man, before turning and leaving the graveyard.

Almost at once Urashima Taro noticed the dates on the newer headstones – it had not been three days since he had last been in this village – it had been almost three hundred years.

"No," he whispered.

As he searched, and the headstones became more aged, he began to notice the names of villagers he had known. Then he came to a weathered slab, located under great tree, and obscured by tall grasses. He pushed the grasses aside and was barely able to read the inscription.

It was his mother's grave. She had died not long after Urashima Taro's last voyage. His name was also written, and underneath it said: Taken by the sea.

Urashima Taro knelt down and wept, and cursed himself bitterly for not listening to his mother when she had implored him not to set sail that stormy evening.

In a fit of despair, he opened the box that Princess Otohime had given him, but to his frustration nothing happened.

He rose and walked back towards the sea in a daze, knowing now that there was nothing for him here and that he should return to the Princess.

Though the beach was not far, he soon found himself beginning to tire. By the time he reached the beach he was barely able to stand, and a moment later he found his legs buckling beneath him. He fell by a rock pool, and when he looked in it he saw his reflection and cried with horror.

Staring back at him was the oldest man he had ever seen, and he could visibly see his reflection – himself – getting older.

He tried to call for the turtle, but his voice barely raised above a croak. He tried again but this time no sound would come. Soon he lay upon the beach and breathed his last, and in less than an hour his body had turned to dust and his ashes were blown out to sea.

And somewhere deep in the ocean Princess Otohime wept.

The Ebony Horse

Introduction

The Ebony Horse was written by an unknown author, possibly of Persian origin circa 900AD, and the tale makes up part of *Arabian Nights*. The ebony horse of the title is a flying machine, upon which Prince Kamar, the story's hero, has a series of adventures.

Rather than simply imbuing the horse with magic, the author used futuristic technology. In this novel story there are mechanisms within the horse, dials to control its flight and it partially inflates before taking off. The ebony horse could therefore be seen not just as a flying machine, but also as a very early portrayal of a robot.

The Ebony Horse

Long ago, there lived a great King called Sabur, and he lived in a splendid palace with his wife, son and three daughters. He was the ruler of all Persia, and was renowned throughout the land for his kindness and wisdom. He was good to his people, comforting those who were distressed, and giving time to those who sought his advice. He also looked after those who had fled from persecution and had sought refuge in his Kingdom. He was hospitable to visitors and generous to the poor, and he was a just man too, with a strong desire to right any wrongs.

Twice a year, Sabur would hold festivals on his palace grounds, once to celebrate the new year, and once to celebrate the Autumn equinox, and people from across Persia, and beyond, would join him to celebrate.

King Sabur was an intelligent man, taking a great interest in science and mathematics, and during one of his festivals he was visited by three inventors who wished to show him their wares.

The first visitor to address him was an Indian, who presented King Sabur with what appeared to be a gold statue, encrusted with gems, and holding a golden trumpet.

"Your Majesty," said the Indian, "this being that I have created will guard your palace against all your enemies. If you place him outside your gates, then when your enemies approach, he will blow the trumpet and your foes will suffer seizures and then death."

The King marvelled at the Indian's work. "If what you have told me is true, then I would happily grant you any wish in return for your creation."

The Indian bowed, and next a Greek inventor came forward. He brought with him a silver dish with a gold peacock in the middle, and twenty four silver chicks about the rim of the dish.

"Oh, mighty King," he began, "as each hour of the day passes, the peacock will turn and peck one of the chicks, so that after one day, all of the chicks will have been pecked. Then, at the end of a lunar month, the peacock will open its beak, and inside you will be able to see the moon."

"That is a fine instrument indeed," said the King, "and I would gladly pay you whatever you asked for it."

The third inventor shuffled forwards. He was an old man of a hundred, with straggling hair and a matted beard. His cheeks were sunken, while his eyes bulged unnaturally. He had three crooked teeth, and in the middle of his wrinkly face was a large, bulbous nose.

He clapped his hands and a horse made of darkest ebony, and inlaid with gold and gemstones trotted into the court. It was fitted with a saddle, bridle and stirrups all made of gold.

"This is my creation," said the old man.

"But how does it walk of its own accord?" asked the King. "Can a person ride it?"

"It can be ridden your Majesty, and not only can my horse trot and canter and gallop – it can fly."

Murmurs broke out through the court, and the Persian craftsman continued. "It can travel through the air, across vast distances and at great speed, and can cover in a single day what others might only be able to in a year."

"By Allah," said the King. "I would give you anything you desire in return for this fine steed."

The King was so impressed by the inventions that he entertained the three wise men for three days, and during that time he witnessed the statue blow its trumpet, and the peacock peck its chicks. The aged Persian inventor mounted the ebony horse and soared high into the air. He flew above the heads of an astonished crowd, before swooping down and landing with ease on the ground.

King Sabur addressed the three sages. "I am amazed by what I have witnessed and believe everything you have told me. Now what gift can I give you in return for your great creations?"

The aged Persian stepped forward and said, "Each of us would like to marry one of your three daughters."

The King did not take long to give his reply. "Your wish is granted."

What neither the King nor the sages knew, was that at this moment the three Princesses were hiding behind a curtain listening to the conversation. The youngest Princess was aghast to hear that she was to be wedded to the ancient Persian, and she ran off to her bedroom, flung herself on her bed, and wept.

Her brother, Prince Kamar, had just returned from a long voyage and knew nothing of the inventors, so as he passed the room of his youngest sister, he was surprised to hear her sobs.

"What's wrong, sister?" he asked.

The Princess sat up, wiped her tears, and recounted her unhappy tale. "Oh brother, I don't wish to marry that horrible old man – but what can I do?"

"I'll talk to father," said Prince Kamar, "and make him see sense."

What neither the Prince nor the Princess knew was at this point the old Persian had overheard their conversation, and scuttled off before the Prince left the room.

Prince Kamar found the King in the open courtyard, and said, "What have you done, father? How can you value a wooden horse above your own daughter?"

The King commanded the servants to bring the horse. "My son," he said, "if you had seen what this horse could do, then you would understand."

The servants brought the horse and Prince Kamar, being an accomplished rider, mounted it, and struck the horse's side with the stirrups.

But the horse did not move. Again the Prince struck the sides of the horse with the stirrups, and again it would not move.

The King called for the inventor, who shuffled into the courtyard.

"Sage," said King Sabur, "show my son how to work this horse."

Having overheard the conversation between the Prince and the Princess, the old man took a dislike to the Prince and now saw an opportunity for revenge.

He approached Prince Kamar. "You see this dial on the right hand side of the horse?"

"Yes," said the Prince.

"You need to turn it."

But no sooner had the Prince done so than the horse shot upwards and vanished from sight.

The King gazed skywards for some time but his son did not return. He ran across to the sage.

"What has happened to my son? Make him return!"

"I cannot, your Majesty," said the sage. "We will not see him now until the Day of Resurrection. Before shooting off into the sky, he was foolish enough not to ask how to land the horse."

The King took off his crown and hurled it at the ground. Then he turned to his guards and pointed at the old man.

"Take him away!" he shouted. "Lock him in jail and throw away the key!"

The King shut himself and his family in the palace, and could not stop his weeping, and when news of this tragedy reached the people of the Kingdom, their happiness turned to grief.

But the Prince was by no means dead. He was soaring through the sky on the ebony horse, in the direction of the sun. Still he could not fathom how to descend.

"There must be a way," he said. "There must!"

He tried the same dial as before, but this only caused the horse to ascend still further and fly at even greater speed. He felt, as far as he was able, over the horse, and found another dial on the horse's left shoulder. With nothing to lose he turned the dial, and the horse began to slow down, and descend towards the Earth.

He found too that the horse had started to respond to

his every touch, the reins turning the horse's head left and right, and causing it to change direction, just like a real horse. Soon Prince Kamar's fear had given way to elation as he realized that he could fly anywhere he wished.

He passed over fields and woods, mountains and rivers, villages and cities, and was amazed by the magnificent views. As the sun was beginning to set, he realized he would never make it home before dark, so he took to setting down in the next town.

Prince Kamar flew over the walls of a splendid city without any of the guards that surrounded it noticing, and he settled the horse on the terrace roof of a palace.

Jumping off the horse, he turned to the wooden creature and said, "The man who made you was a clever man indeed – and a cunning one too. Let us hope that we are able to return home soon."

The sky was now inky blue, and the first few stars beginning to twinkle. Having not had anything to eat or drink since the morning, Prince Kamar left the horse, descended a nearby staircase, and found himself in a fine courtyard paved with marble.

It was deserted and eerily quiet. He wandered along the moonlit path around the palace's perimeter. After a minute of walking he noticed a chink of light and saw that a palace side-door was ajar.

Leaning against the door frame was a eunuch, guarding the entrance, but as Prince Kamar approached he heard the guard's soft snores. The Prince took the sleeping guard's sword, snuck inside, and found some food and water which he devoured gratefully. Being of an adventurous spirit, the Prince ventured further inside the palace.

Sneaking through one of the many doors, he entered a room where, in the middle, he saw four servant girls lying around a bed of ivory and jewels.

The Prince crept past the servant girls and saw that on the bed lay a beautiful young woman. She had fair skin, and soft red cheeks, and was so beautiful that Kamar could not help but lean over and kiss her.

Her eyes opened.

"Who are you?" she asked.

"I am your love, and your slave," said the Prince.

"You must be the suitor whom my father rejected," said the lady, rubbing her eyes. "My father said you were an ugly and unpleasant man, but you seem to be neither of those."

The slaves awoke to see their mistress talking to the stranger.

"Princess – who is this man?" one of them asked.

"I don't know," said the young woman. "When I awoke, he was seated by my bed. I believe he is the suitor my father rejected."

"No," replied the slave girl. "I saw your suitor – he looked like some grotesque creature, and his manners were terrible."

The four maidens went outside and saw the eunuch sleeping. They woke him and said, "how did you let a men get through and wake us from our sleep?"

The eunuch ran inside and shouted at the Prince. "How did you sneak past me?" he blustered. "Did you bewitch me? Are you some sort of demon?"

"How dare you compare me to such an evil creature. I am your King's son-in-law. I have married his daughter, and he has asked me to visit her."

The eunuch frowned. "I beg your pardon, my lord," said the eunuch. "I meant no disrespect."

Blushing, the eunuch retreated and then ran to the King.

Suspicious of the Prince's words, the eunuch told the King of what he had seen. "You will need to rescue your daughter from this evil demon, this abomination that has taken on the appearance of a handsome and noble man."

"You fool," said the King. "How did you let him slip past?"

"He must have bewitched me, sire."

The King marched to his daughter's bedroom, and addressed the servant girls.

"What has become of my daughter?" he asked.

"Your Majesty," they replied, "sleep overcame us all, and when we woke we saw a young man sitting on the edge of Princess Shams bed, and talking to her. We asked him who he was, and he said that you had given him your daughter's hand in marriage. We knew nothing of this, and we did not know if he was a man or a spirit, but he is modest and well-bred, and has done nothing untoward."

When the King heard this, his anger cooled, and he passed through a curtain into an adjacent room where his daughter was sitting, talking to the Prince.

Once more the King's anger grew and, unable to control his temper, he charged at the Prince, who leapt up, sword in hand.

"Is this your father?" Prince Kamar asked the lady.

"Yes," she replied.

The King was no match for the Prince, and in the end the King, knowing he could not defeat the youth, put his sword back in its sheath.

"Young man," he said. "Are you the noble man that you appear to be, or are you some evil spirit who has bewitched my household?"

"If I was a demon, I would not have spared you. I am Prince Kamar, son of King Sabur of Persia."

"But if you are a noble Prince, then how did you enter my palace? Why did you come without an invitation, or even request to be invited? Why did you enter my daughter's room, and why did you say that I had given you her hand in marriage? And if I called out now and my guards came rushing in, who would be able to save you from a dozen sharp swords? Who could save you?"

"Do you think that someone as brave as handsome as I am, is unworthy of marriage to your daughter?"

"It is not just about looks and bravery. Your coming here, to my daughter's room, in such a manner, is hardly befitting of a Prince."

"That is true, but calling your guards and having them kill me will only cause great trouble for you. People will surely ask what I was doing in your daughter's bedroom. And while many may believe what you say, many will not. So let me give you some words of wisdom."

The King folded his arms. "Pray tell," he said.

"You could fight me in armed combat, here and now, or I could take on your entire army. But first you will need to tell me how many men you have."

"More than forty thousand."

"Tomorrow morning you can tell them that they must take me on. Tell them also that if I am slain, so be it, and if I rout them, then I am to have your daughter's hand in marriage. If I am slain, the secret is taken to my grave, and if I succeed, then any King should be happy to have me as his son-in-law."

The King thought for a few moments, and then accepted Prince Kamar's proposition.

The next morning, as the soldiers put on their armour and mounted their horses, the Prince and the King spoke at length. The King found Prince Kamar to be an intelligent man and of good breeding, and as the Prince left to do battle, the King said: "Take any of my horses that you wish."

"The only horse I shall ride into battle, is the one that brought me here."

"And where is this horse?"

"Your palace."

"Don't be absurd," said the King. "If your horse was there, my guards would have told me. Whereabouts in the palace?"

"Up on the roof."

"Are you mocking me, Prince? Well, no matter, we shall see." The King turned to one of his generals. "Go to the palace roof and bring me anything you might find."

The people nearest were amazed by the very notion. "How could a horse have ascended the steps?" they asked. "How on Earth will anyone be able to lead it back down?"

The soldier took some of his men with him and they soon found the horse. When they realised it was made of ebony and not a real horse, they laughed.

"Is this the horse he rode into town?" said the general.

"We'll soon find out," said one of the soldiers, and together they lifted the horse and carried it down the steps.

When they set it down before the King, he marvelled at the workmanship.

"Prince Kamar," he said, "is this really your horse?"

"It is, your majesty, and soon I will show it to you in all its glory."

"Very well," said the King, "mount your horse."

"Not until your troops withdraw some way from it."

The King ordered his troops to withdraw so far that the horse was just out of the bowmen's range.

"Do not spare the lives of any of my men," said the King, "for they certainly will not spare yours."

Prince Kamar leapt onto his horse and sat facing an almost uncountable number of soldiers.

They stared back at this solitary figure.

"When he comes near, we can run him through with our pikes, and then chop him to pieces with our swords," said one soldier.

"It doesn't seem right, slaying that young man," said another.

"I don't think slaying him will be that easy – he managed to get into the city and then into the palace without so much as a scratch."

The Prince slowly turned the ascent dial. The horse shuddered, and Prince Kamar saw the creature's belly fill with air. He and his steed began to rise, slowly at first, and then Kamar and the horse shot up into the sky.

The King cried aloud. "Chase after him – he didn't want the horse to fight a battle, he wanted it to escape!"

Prince Kamar flew out over the city walls, waving as he left.

"Follow him!" the King ordered, as the Prince flew away.

But his council of wise men said, "There is no way the Prince and his flying horse can be caught. Look, he's already but a speck on the horizon. He is surely a mighty wizard – be thankful he has left without using his powers upon you and your subjects."

The King returned to his palace and explained what had happened to his daughter.

Princess Shams broke down, and began to sob.

The King put his arms round the Princess and tried to console her.

"There, there, my daughter," he said. "Be thankful that we are free from this deceitful sorcerer who came here to seduce you. Remember all the lies he spoke – do not let your heart break over such a scoundrel."

But Princess Shams would not listen to her father. "I will not eat and I will not drink until I meet with my Prince once more."

"My daughter, do not speak of such things."

But the more the King tried to talk to his daughter, the stronger her love grew for the Prince.

At this moment Prince Kamar rejoiced at having escaped, and felt exhilarated as he flew through the air. But his joy was dampened when he thought of the beautiful Princess he had left behind. On the way home he landed and enquired about the city he had left, and was told its name was Sana.

The journey home seemed quicker than his unplanned trip to Sana, and when he saw his father's capital, his heart filled with joy. He circled round the city before alighting on the palace roof.

He descended the steps, and saw ashes strewn across the entrance – a sign that someone in the family had died. He entered to see his mother, father and sisters dressed in black, consoling one another.

The King turned and saw his son.

"No," said the King, "it cannot be!"

Soon Prince Kamar found himself being embraced by all his family. They had all thought him dead and were overjoyed that their mourning had been unnecessary.

Prince Kamar recounted his adventure to his happy family, and the King decided to hold a great festival across Persia to celebrate his son's return. The population cast off their mourning clothes, and dressed themselves in their most colourful garments. Streets were decorated, and parties were held in every town. The King proclaimed that all prisoners should be pardoned, and every prisoner in the country was released, and for seven days and nights celebrations took place across the land.

He and his son took their finest horses and rode through towns and villages, so the people might see the Prince.

"What became of the sage who created the ebony horse?" asked the Prince.

"I threw him in prison, but as you are alive and well, I shall release him as I have released all prisoners."

After they had spent the day riding through joyous crowds, they returned to the palace, and the King sent for the sage. The old man was treated with utmost kindness, and was given food and drink and new clothes.

"Your Highness, I was promised that I could marry your daughter –"

"Hold your tongue," said the King. "You will not marry her after what you did to my son. Be thankful that you are no longer in chains."

"But you made a promise!" the sage cried. "Your daughter should now be my wife!"

"Get him out," said the King, and two soldiers dragged the old sage, and threw him out of the palace gates, then locked them so he could not get back in.

"My son," said the King, "you would do well to steer clear of that man's strange horse. I doubt you know all of its capabilities, and I can hardly bear the thought of you flying away again."

The Prince told his father about the King of Sana, and Princess Shams, and felt the pang of separation as he spoke of her. A female singer took to performing in front of the royal family and their guests. She played her stringed instrument with great skill, and when she sang of separated lovers, the Prince asked that he might leave the room for a while.

Prince Kamar was overwhelmed with yearning for his distant Princess, and he decided, in spite of what his father had told him, that he had to see her again.

He ascended the steps to the palace roof and

mounted his black wooden horse. He turned the ascent dial, and soon he was in the air, flying back towards the city he had only recently escaped.

The next morning the King realized his son had disappeared once more, and after a quick search of the castle it was found that the horse had gone too.

"If my son comes back to me," the King said to himself, "I'll make sure I destroy that infernal horse." And he broke down and wept.

The Prince though was in a cheery mood, and he did not stop at any point on his long flight until he reached the city of Sana, and once more alighted on the palace roof. He crept down the stairs and past the eunuch who was asleep again. When he reached the door to Princess Sana's bedroom, Prince Kamar heard her weeping.

One of the servant girls said, "Why do you mourn for a someone who never loved you?"

But the Princess continued to cry, and Prince Kamar could not remain outside the room a moment longer.

"Why do you weep, my love?" said the Prince.

Princess Sana, threw her arms about the Prince and kissed him. "I thought I would never see you again," she replied.

"I had to come back and see you," said the Prince.

"If you had stayed away a day longer," said Princess Shams, "I think I would have died of grief."

"I hope your father does not try to come between us," said Prince Kamar. "Had it not been for my love for you, I would have run him through with my sword."

"Why did you leave me, my love?"

"I had to, but only for a while. Let us not dwell on such things now, I'm hungry and thirsty."

The servant girls brought him food and drink, and he and Princess Shams sat talking well into the night.

When dawn broke, the Prince said, "I should leave before the eunuch guard wakes."

"Where will you go?" said the Princess.

"Back to my father's palace," the Prince replied, and on seeing the dismay and sadness in her eyes, added. "I will come back to see you every week, and I pledge now that you will be my only love, always and forever."

But his words could not stem her weeping. "Why not take me with you?"

"Would you do that?" he replied. "Would you come with me back to my father's palace?"

"My life is worthless without you," said the Princess. "Please let me come."

"Then let us not waste another moment," said the Prince.

Princess Shams adorned herself with her most cherished jewels, said goodbye to her maidens, and followed Prince Kamar onto the palace roof. She sat on the ebony horse, behind the Prince, and put her arms tightly about his waist. Prince Kamar turned the ascent dial, and soon they were rising into the air.

When the maidens saw their mistress flying off, they were so shocked that they cried aloud and ran to tell Princess Shams' mother and father. The King and Queen ran outside to see their daughter flying away, and the King cried aloud. "In the name of Allah, bring our daughter back to us you evil spirit!"

The Prince, worried that the Princess might be having second thoughts, said, "Do you wish me to return you to your parents?"

"No – fly on!" replied the Princess. "My only wish is to be with you."

The Prince flew the horse at a moderate pace, so as not to frighten the Princess, and they alighted in a green field where a fresh water river cut through. They sat and ate and drank, and after they had rested, they took off once more, flying on until they could see King Sabur's palace.

Prince Kamar could not wait to show Princess Shams the splendour of his father's Kingdom, and the beautiful palace where his family lived, and when he approached one of his father's gardens, just outside the city, he turned the descent dial so they floated downwards and landed softly.

"Wait here, my love," said the Prince, leaving the Princess and the ebony horse. "I will let my father know you have come, and I will send a servant to escort you inside when everything is ready."

The Princess understood that as a member of a royal family, she should not enter the city without first being invited by the King.

The King was glad to see his son safe and well, and said nothing of his sadness at his son having left the palace.

"I have brought Princess Shams with me," said the Prince. "She is outside the city walls in one of your gardens. I hope you will welcome her to our city."

"With all my heart!" exclaimed the King, and he collected the most important people within the city and together they rode out to welcome the Princess.

Meanwhile the Prince set up decorations within the palace and gathered together servant girls to tend to all Princess Shams' needs. Then he set out to join his father and his love. But when he reached the gardens Princess Shams was not there. She had disappeared, and so had the horse.

"What has happened?" he said to his father. "Where is she?"

"The guards say that the Persian sage came through the entrance to collect herbs, but never left the garden as far as they could tell."

"He's taken her!" cried the Prince. "I will search for her, and I'll not come back until I have found her again."

"But you will never be able to find her," said the King. "Come home with us now. Do not spend the rest of your life searching in vain."

But the Prince would not listen to his father. His feelings for Princess Sana were far too strong.

When the Prince had left the Princess in the garden, the sage, quite by chance had gone there to collect herbs, as the guards had reported. His bulbous nose gave him a keen sense of smell, and when he sniffed the air he could sense some exquisite perfumes. So he followed his nose, until he spied the Princess standing by the horse that he had built.

He had mourned the loss of his horse and thought, until now, that he would never see it again. Now his heart leapt with delight. He approached the Princess, who could not help but shrink back at the sight of such a hideous looking man.

"Who are you?" she asked.

The sage knew she was of royal blood by her countenance, and that she must be waiting to be let into the city.

"I am a messenger, my lady," he said. "Prince Kamar has asked me to escort you into the city."

"Could he have not found someone more handsome to escort me?" she said.

"The Prince sent the ugliest servant he could find because he has a jealous nature," said the sage, "and thought that if he sent someone more handsome, you might elope."

They talked some more, and the cunning sage was able to convince the Princess that she had made a grave mistake in coming here with the Prince.

"You should leave here as quickly as possible," said the old man. "Or you will face a life of utter misery, just like his other wives."

"But how shall we leave?"

"On this horse."

"But I do not know how to fly it."

"Do not worry yourself, my lady," said the sage, "I know how to control its movements."

So the old man sat on the horse, and Princess Shams sat behind him, and soon they were flying through the air.

It suddenly dawned on the Princess that the Prince would be unlikely to send a man who would so easily betray him.

"Why did you disobey your Prince?" she asked.

"He is not my Prince," snapped the old man. "He is little more than a well-dressed snake. Do you know who I am?"

"No – I thought you were one of the Prince's servants."

"Well I'm not his servant and never have been. He's an arrogant young upstart, and his father is a wicked and unjust man, who stole my horse and threw me in prison."

"Your horse – the one we're riding now?"

"Of course," said the sage. "I made it myself and thought I'd lost it forever. But now I have it back, and I have you, and I hope it causes the Prince and his family more suffering than they caused me. You shall be my wife, in place of the King's daughter. Your life will not be a bad one if you marry me. I am clever and I am wealthy, and I have plenty of slaves that will serve you."

"Take me back to the Prince at once!"

But the Sage took no notice, he wasn't going to lose a wife for a second time.

Princess Shams wept for the whole journey, until they reached Greece and alighted in a meadow filled with streams and trees. In the not too far distance was a beautiful city where a King lived, and it happened that at this moment, the King was out hunting and saw the old sage and the Princess.

The King's servants brought the Princess and the old man to their master.

The King eyed the ugly old sage and the beautiful young Princess.

"What is the relationship between you?" the King asked the sage. "Is she your granddaughter?"

"What should you care?" growled the sage. "Just

because you're dressed in all your finery you think you can harass a poor old man." said the sage. "Well if you really must know, she is my wife, and, as it happens, the daughter of my father's brother."

"He is not my husband!" the Princess exclaimed. "He's a wicked old man, who has kidnapped me!"

The King believed the Princess, and the Persian sage was beaten by the King's soldiers, taken back to the King's city and thrown into jail. Then the King escorted the Princess and the ebony horse back to his palace.

Prince Kamar grabbed some money and all that he needed to travel, and set off in search of his beloved Princess. He journeyed from city to city and from country to country, asking people if they had seen Princess Shams or the ebony horse. But all his searches and questions appeared to be in vain – no one could give him even a scrap of information. He even visited the Princess's father, but even here there was no news, and so Prince Kamar left the mourning King.

The Prince, having covered the whole of Persia, and having had no luck, made for Greece, where his enquiries at last proved fruitful.

It happened that he came across a group of merchants, who were talking among themselves.

"You'll never believe what I saw," said one of them.

"Come on," said another. "Tell us."

"I was visiting the King's city, and heard the strangest tale. The King was out hunting when he came to a green meadow, and came across an ugly old man, a beautiful young woman and an ebony horse."

"And then what?"

"The old man claimed that the woman was his wife and cousin, but she told the King that the old man was lying and that he'd kidnapped her. The King threw the old man in jail, but I couldn't tell you what became of the young woman or the ebony horse."

Prince Kamar approached the storyteller.

"Pray, tell me the name of this city and where I might find it," he asked.

The merchant happily gave the Prince all the information that was requested, but as it was late the Prince stayed at some lodgings and did not set off until first light the following morning.

After a few hours travel on his trusty horse, Prince Kamar reached the entrance to the King's metropolis. The gatekeepers had been told by the King to bring him any stranger that might visit the city, and so they escorted Prince Kamar to the palace. Here the King would normally ask any stranger to state their reason for visiting, but on this occasion the King was dining and would not be disturbed, so the gatekeepers put the Prince in the hands of the prison guards.

The guards could not believe that such a handsome and refined young man could mean any harm, so they let him dine with them.

"Where are you from?" one of the guards asked.

"Persia," the Prince replied. "From the land of the Chosroes."

The guard laughed. "Well that's a coincidence – you're not the only Chosroan in this prison."

"It's true," said the other guard. "There's an ugly old man, who was probably just as ugly when he was young. Everything he says is either unpleasant, or a downright lie."

"What lies has he told?"

"He said he was a wise man. When the King found him in a meadow, the old man was with a beautiful young lady and an ebony horse. He said the woman was his wife, when she wasn't. It turns out he'd kidnapped her, and so the King threw him in prison."

"What has become of the Princess?" said Prince Kamar.

The guard shook his head. "She's gone mad. The King wants to marry her, but can't so long as she's in this state. The old man was asked to cure her, but he couldn't. The King has employed the finest physicians and astrologers to cure her, but no one's been able."

The other guard spoke: "The horse is somewhere in the King's palace. The old man is here with us in the prison, and at night he wails and cries so loudly that we're kept awake until dawn."

When it was time to sleep, the Prince allowed himself to be escorted back to his prison cell, and he lay upon a bed of straw. The guards locked him in, and bade him goodnight.

Soon, just as the guards had said, he heard the Persian sage weeping and crying aloud.

"What a fool I've been!" he sobbed. "Why did I steal that beautiful young woman away when I knew I had no chance of making her my wife? I have left the Prince without the woman he loves, and now I'm stuck in this miserable place! Oh, what have I done?"

The Prince called back. "Old sage," he shouted. "How long are you going to weep for? Do you think that you are the only person who suffers? There are others who have a harder time than you, but do not complain of their lot."

Still the sage moaned, but the Prince, to his own surprise, began to pity the ugly old man.

The next morning the Prince was taken from his cell and directly to the King.

"Where are you from," asked the King, "and why have you come here?"

"My name is Harjah" said Prince Kamar, "and I am from Persia. I am a wise man who travels around healing the sick, especially those who have been possessed and driven to madness by malevolent spirits. To this day I have never failed to heal a patient."

The King clapped his hands delightedly. "Sage," he exclaimed, "you do not know what happiness your words have brought me! Never has a person come at a more appropriate time. Praise be to Allah!"

The King then told Prince Kamar about the Princess and her affliction.

"If you cure her, I shall give you anything you want."

"Let us hope that Allah looks upon this case favourably," said the Prince. "Tell me all you know of her affliction, how long she has suffered from it, and how she came to be with the horse and the old man."

The King recounted the whole story faithfully, in every detail.

"And where is the old man now?" asked the Prince.

"He is in jail."

"And what about the ebony horse?"

"It has been stowed away in one of my treasure chambers."

"First, I will need to see the horse and check its condition," said the Prince. "If it is in good condition I believe it can help the poor young woman."

"Yes, of course," said the King. "I can take you to see the horse immediately."

"Lead the way," said the Prince.

So the King led the Prince to the treasure chamber. Prince Kamar examined the horse in minute detail, as the King looked on.

"It seems fine," the Prince said at last. "Let us go and visit the damsel, and see if we can cure her."

So together they visited the Princess, who was in her bedroom. The Prince saw her sitting on the ground, rocking back and forth, crying, and beating the ground with her fists. Then she began to claw at her dress and rip it shreds. But she was not mad, she feigned this affliction so that people – not least the King – would be too scared to approach her.

"I mean you no harm," said Prince Kamar, not knowing if she really was insane.

Through her tears and distress the Princess did not realize that it was the Prince who addressed her.

When he knelt by her side he whispered in her ear. "It is I, Prince Kamar."

The moment Princess Shams heard these words she cried out and fainted.

The King thought the Princess had, through fear of the stranger, suffered a seizure.

The Prince picked her up and said as quietly as possible. "Shams, I hope you can hear me. I've come to help you escape from the King. I have told him I am a sage who has come to cure you. I will tell him that to

139

drive away the spirit that possesses you, he will first have to let you leave his castle. I want you speak to him kindly whenever he talks to you, so that he thinks that I've cured you."

She opened her eyes. "Very well my love," she said, and sat up.

"Your majesty," said the Prince, " I have discovered the cause of her disease, and have cured her. Come and talk to her with kindness. There will be a little more to do, but I believe the worst is over."

The King approached her with caution, but when she looked up and saw him, Princess Shams smiled.

"Thank you for visiting me," she said.

The King, seeing that she was no longer raving, felt his heart skip with joy, and he bade his servants to escort her to a better room and dress her in the finest clothes and jewellery.

As she was bathed by female servants, she made polite conversation with them, then she was dressed and adorned with beautiful jewels. Then she was escorted to the King where she kissed the ground before him.

"Wise sage!" the King said happily, "You have done a great deed! I must be the happiest person in the Kingdom!"

"There is still more work to be done," Prince Kamar said solemnly. "Bring me the ebony horse," he said. "The spirit that possessed this woman, came from that horse and has undoubtedly returned there. Unless I banish the spirit from the horse, he will return and possess the woman once more."

"I will do it at once," said the King, and he

commanded his servants to bring the horse.

"We shall all go to the meadow where you found her," said the Prince.

So the King, Prince Kamar and Princess Shams rode out to the meadow, while the servants carried the ebony horse.

The Prince turned to the King. "This will be a dangerous affair," he said grimly. "You and the servants will need to keep well back."

"How far?" asked the King.

"Until we are specks in the distance," said the Prince. "I will have to banish the spirit, and then imprison him so that he can never harm another human being. Then I will have to mount the horse with the lady. After this the horse will begin to rock, then it will fly through the air towards you, and then all shall be well and you can do as you wish with the damsel."

So the King retreated so he could barely see what what was going on. He saw the Prince and Princess mount the ebony horse, then he saw them take off into the sky. For half a day he waited for them to return, and then he began to grieve.

Frustrated at being duped, he returned to the palace with his servants, and summoned the old man.

"You treacherous swine! Why didn't you tell me the properties of the ebony horse!" he cried. "Now a man even more cunning you has taken the horse, and the woman I loved. And if that wasn't bad enough, she was wearing some of the finest jewels that my soldiers have plundered!"

The old man recounted the whole tale truthfully from beginning to end, and in his despair the King suffered a seizure that almost ended his life.

The King was taken to his bed chamber and over the next few days, with the aid of his physicians, he eventually recovered.

"Sire," said one of his wise men, "be thankful that you are rid of that woman who undoubtedly was some sort of witch, and praise Allah that the sorcerer that took her away did no more damage."

Eventually these soothing words comforted the King, and soon he was happily seeking out a new bride.

The Prince and Princess flew back to Persia, and to King Sabur's palace. They alighted on the roof, and Prince Kamar left the Princess in the company of the horse.

He found his mother and father and together they rejoiced at their reunion, then the Prince explained that he had brought Princess Shams with him, and they were cheered to hear that he had found his love and had brought her back with him.

Great banquets were laid out for all the people of the capital, and there were celebrations for a whole month, culminating in the marriage of the royal couple.

King Sabur smashed the ebony horse, breaking all the mechanisms within it that gave it the ability to fly, and though Prince Kamar was sad to see this, he understood why it had been done.

Prince Kamar wrote to the Princess's father, explaining the whole tale and telling him of the marriage, and he sent a messenger along with some very fine gifts. When the messenger reached the city of Sana, and delivered the gifts and the letter, the King was rejoiced to hear that his daughter was happy and well. He gathered together gifts of his own and gave them to the messenger to take to his daughter and son-in-law.

Every year Prince Kamar would send the King letters and gifts, and in time Prince Kamar became King, and Princess Shams became Queen, and, just as King Sabur had done, they ruled together justly and wisely for the rest of their lives.

The City of Brass

Introduction

The City of Brass was written by an unknown author, possibly of Persian origin circa 900AD, and the story makes up part of *Arabian Nights*. In this tale a group of travellers come upon a walled ghost town with no discernible entrance. When they are eventually able to enter the city, among their strange encounters, they come across automata and a mummified queen. This is a fantasy tale in the main, but is included in this anthology as it contains some elements of science fiction.

The City of Brass

Long ago there lived a Caliph by the name of Malik. He was very interested in myths and legends, and one day, while talking with kings and sultans, their conversation turned to an old tale of how King Solomon had managed to imprison spirits and demons in stoppered bottles.

A young man named Talib, who was present in this conversation, knew of this tale and said, "My grandfather once captained a ship that was blown far off course by a great storm. They ran aground and after journeying for some months, they reached the foot of some great mountains. Here they came across a tribe of black-skinned people. None of them spoke Arabic, but fortunately, the king of the tribe was sent for, and he was able to converse a little with my grandfather. The king welcomed the crew and entertained them for three days. On the fourth day, my grandfather was taken fishing, but among the fish contained in one particular net was a blue, stoppered bottle. The fishermen and my grandfather returned to shore, where a sailor smashed the bottle against some rocks, shattering it into a thousand pieces. A genie billowed out, looking like smoke, and grew until he was as high as the clouds.

"'Oh, Allah!' the Genie cried. 'Allah, I am sorry for all the wickedness I have done!'

"After that, the genie disappeared. The king told my

grandfather and his crew that local fishermen often dredged up these bottles, and broke them open to release some repenting spirit."

The Caliph was amazed by Talib's strange tale.

"Talib," he said, "you must travel to Morocco and meet with Musa the Emir, and together you shall go on a journey to seek out these strange bottles."

So Talib made the long journey to Morocco and met with Musa, where he explained the Caliph's wish. Talib and Musa the Emir set off in the company of a wise Sheikh called Samad, and took with them plenty of men, camels and provisions.

The Sheikh had heard of this legend and had some idea of the way to the base of these great mountains by the sea. He explained that they should follow the coast, and that the journey should take around four months.

To begin with they made good progress, with the Sheikh using the stars to plot their journey. But after a few cloudy nights, when none of the stars could be seen, they wandered off course.

For days they saw nothing, and their first sight of human habitation was a great, bejewelled palace.

"My grandfather also came across a palace like this one," said Talib, "and after this he came across another place called the City of Brass, which he was unable to enter."

The bejewelled palace was deserted, and the Sheikh read a scroll that explained how Death had visited this wondrous place. The king at the time had tried to bargain with Death, offering up all his treasures for one more day of life. But Death would not bargain, and the king died at his appointed time.

So Talib, the Emir, the Sheikh and their men left the palace, and continued their journey across the barren lands. After a few days of monotony they saw, in the distance, a man on his horse, and they decided to approach him. But he was no ordinary man. Indeed he wasn't really a man at all, for he, and his horse, were made of brass.

At the base of this metal statue some words were inscribed:

'Touch the hand of this rider, and he will point you in the direction of the City of Brass.'

Talib touched the hot metal hand. A moment passed when all was still and quiet, then a creaking noise sounded. The horse turned as though on a revolving plate, then stopped. The rider's arm raised stiffly, and his finger pointed.

Leaving this mysterious statue, the party took the direction given to them by the horseman, and after a journey of many days they came to the city.

"Where is the entrance?" asked the Emir, looking up and along the city's high, golden wall.

Talib took a company of twenty five men round the entire perimeter, and after three days they returned, full circle, back to their companions.

"We've searched every part of the wall," said Talib. "There is no way in. It doesn't make sense."

"I have heard," said the Sheikh that there are twenty five portals, none of which can be opened from outside the city."

"Then how are we supposed to enter?" said Talib.

The Sheikh replied, "I do not know."

"If we cannot go through," said the Emir, "then

perhaps we could try going over the top. We have enough materials to make a tall ladder."

Over the next few days a tall, sturdy ladder was made, then lifted and lent against the city wall.

There were no shortage of volunteers to climb the ladder and see if there was any way down into the city. Eventually one soldier, renowned for his courage and ability, was allowed to climb to the top of the city wall.

"What can you see?" called the Emir.

But the soldier did not reply. He just stared down into the city with a faint smile on his face – and then he jumped, screaming as he fell.

"The journey must have taken its toll on him more than we ever suspected," said Talib.

A second soldier was sent up the ladder, and he too stood at the top of the wall, staring down the other side.

"What do you see?" shouted the Emir.

The soldier, like the last, did not reply, and before anyone could act, the man jumped into the city to the horror of his companions.

A third soldier was sent up and he too jumped to his death, and so it continued until a dozen soldiers had perished in the same manner.

"Let me go next," said the Sheikh.

"No," said the Emir, "absolutely not. If we lose you, our quest is at an end."

"I promise you, Emir, Allah will not desert me."

Eventually, after much discussion, the Emir allowed the old Sheikh to ascend the ladder.

As he climbed, the Sheikh prayed all the while, and

when he reached the top of the wall, he stepped upon the wide metal plateau, and gazed down into the city.

Below, there was a deep lake of water, or so it seemed, shimmering and glistening in the sunlight. Around the edge of the lake were twelve beautiful maidens, encouraging him to jump into the cool, sparkling lake. But the Sheikh resisted their tempting calls, and as he continued to pray, the lake began to fade, and he could see the broken bodies of the twelve soldiers.

Knowing they could not tempt him, the maidens vanished, and the lake disappeared. The Sheikh walked along the wide top of the wall until he came to a turret with no visible entrance. In front of the wall was a brass horseman, not unlike the one that had directed the Sheikh and his companions to the City of Brass. There was an inscription at the base of this metal statue:

'Whoever wishes to enter the City of Brass must turn the dial in the middle of my chest twelve times.'

There was a dial and with some effort the Sheikh turned it. The Sheikh stepped back as sparks began to fly, and the horseman began to rotate. As it turned a door began to open.

The Sheikh passed through the entrance, and descended a staircase until he found himself in a dusty old room, filled with skeletons. On the wall was a set of keys, which he took. He left the room and walked along the inside of the city wall until he came to a great brass door, which he knew to be quite invisible from the other side.

He put the largest key in the lock and turned it. The

door, of its own accord, began to creak open, and soon the Sheikh was face-to-face with his companions once more.

As they explored the city, they found not a living soul. They found many skeletons dressed in rags, there were skeletons in the houses and in the market place, as though Death had come swiftly to the city and caught its inhabitants off guard.

Talib, the Emir, the Sheikh and a handful of soldiers entered one particularly fine building, a palace made of gold and silver. Inside there were beautifully carved pieces of furniture, draped in silk, and there were fine paintings and ornaments made of the most precious gems. They explored the whole building and were amazed by the treasures they saw. But when they came to the end of one long, wide corridor, they found that the door would not open. It was a particularly fine door made of ebony and inlaid with gold. The Emir looked at the door, but there seemed to be no way of opening it and there appeared to be no lock. The Sheikh spent some time putting his hands on different parts of the door. He said that he knew what he was doing, and eventually the door clicked open.

The small group passed into what was undoubtedly the most splendid room in the palace. It was made of marble, and much of the stone was decorated with sapphires and diamonds and emeralds. There was a bird made of rubies, and on the couch lay a young woman. Of all the jewels in the city, the finest adorned her. She wore a silk robe, inlaid with pearls, a red-gold crown sparkling with gems, a jewelled amulet on her breast, and a necklace of rubies and emeralds. To her left and right, flanking her couch, were two statues of slaves, one black and one white, and each with a sword in his hand.

At first the Emir thought the young woman was still alive, but Talib was less certain.

"She has been mummified," said the Sheikh. "Mercury was put behind her eyes to make them glisten, and the air blows her eyelashes, giving them a sense of movement."

In the woman's hand was a piece of paper, which the Sheikh took and read aloud to his companions.

"Welcome to those whom Allah has let into my city. Take any treasure you wish, but pray leave those treasures that adorn me."

"But she is dead," said Talib, staring longingly at the glittering jewels the dead young woman wore. "She has no need of them now."

Before anyone could stop him, Talib stepped forwards and reached out to grab the woman's crown. The moment his fingers touched it, the black statue swung his sword and sliced Talib's head clean off.

"Come," said the Sheikh, "let us leave this place. We still have the Caliph's task to complete."

The Emir and the soldiers loaded their camels with treasures from the City of Brass, and continued their journey. After a month of travelling, they came across some mountains overlooking the sea. They were welcomed by black-skinned people who lived there and spoke a quite different language. The king of these people, however, was able to speak Arabic, and he conversed with the Sheikh and the Emir.

The Emir said, "We have been sent by Malik the

Caliph, to find bottles in which King Solomon imprisoned demons and spirits. We have journeyed many months in the hope of finding these items."

"Then you have reached your destination," said the king.

He showed his guests great hospitality, letting them rest for many days. After a week, his fishermen had managed to find a dozen such bottles, which the Emir and Sheikh took back to the Caliph.

The Caliph, upon receiving the bottles, smashed some of them open, releasing many repentant spirits. Then he sent more men to the City of Brass, to recover treasures, which he divided among the faithful.

The Tale of the Bamboo Cutter

Introduction

The Tale of the Bamboo Cutter was written by an unknown Japanese author around the tenth century AD. This beautiful tale, blending romance and science fiction, tells of a girl found as a baby amongst some bamboo. As she grows, she reveals that she is a Princess exiled from the Moon. Eventually her people come in their spacecraft to take her home. This is the earliest known story to tell of extraterrestrials visiting the Earth.

The Tale of the Bamboo Cutter

Long ago there lived an old bamboo cutter. He and his wife were very poor, and to their dismay they had never been blessed with children. The old man toiled each day in his bamboo field, earning just enough to live on by cutting down and selling the shoots.

One evening however, when his day's toil was coming to a close, he noticed a fabulous light shining nearby. Hacking his way through the shoots, he soon came across the source of this strange glow – a baby girl, small enough to fit on the palm of his hand. The bamboo cutter picked up the girl and took her home. He and his wife were delighted at the prospect of raising the child, and they blessed the girl with the name Lady Kaguya.

From this day, whenever the bamboo cutter went into his field to work, he found a small nugget of gold in every stalk that he cut, and within a month he and his wife had become very rich. But this was not the only strange occurrence, for Lady Kaguya developed at such speed, that after just a few months she had grown to the height of an ordinary human. She was also very beautiful, and she was soon reckoned to be the prettiest young woman in the country, causing men from far and wide to come and see her for themselves.

The bamboo cutter soon became wearied by the young men's demands to see Lady Kaguya, and his attempts to send them away only met with limited success. While other men relented, five noblemen could not be persuaded to leave, and all pleaded with the bamboo cutter to let them marry his beautiful daughter. The bamboo cutter explained that as she was not really his child, it was up to her whether or not she wished to marry any of them.

Eventually Lady Kaguya agreed to meet the five noblemen. She set each of them a near-impossible task, and said that she would marry the first man to complete his task successfully.

The first nobleman was told that he must travel to India and bring back a stone begging bowl that had been used by Buddha himself; the second nobleman was told he must travel to a distant land where he had to find a tree with gold branches, silver roots, and fruit of pure jade, and bring Lady Kaguya one of the tree's branches; the third was asked to find a magical robe made from the pelts of flame-proof rats; the fourth was told to retrieve a jewel that lay buried in the heart of an infamous dragon, and the fifth was asked to bring back a cowry-shell born from swallows.

For years, the five men ventured across the known world to compete their quests. The first nobleman eventually realised the impossible nature of his task and forged the bowl, before presenting it to Lady Kaguya. She took the bowl from him, but when night came she saw that it did not glow with holy light and, realising that the nobleman had tried to deceive her, told him he had failed in his quest.

The second nobleman also tried to forge the golden branch he had been asked to retrieve, but he too was found out. The third and fourth noblemen fared no better and, eventually realizing the folly of their pursuit, gave up on their quests, while the fifth, in search of the strange cowry-shell, lost his life in a far off land.

News of Lady Kaguya eventually reached the Emperor and he sent one of his maids to meet with this mysterious young woman. Lady Kaguya, however, refused to meet with the Emperor's messenger. The Emperor then sent a letter to the bamboo cutter and his daughter, inviting them to his palace, and offering to bestow a noble title upon the old man. The bamboo cutter was overjoyed by the offer, but his happiness faded when he saw the look on his daughter. Lady Kaguya looked at him sadly, and explained that if she ever left his house she would die.

So the bamboo cutter travelled to the palace alone, and explained the situation to the Emperor. Intrigued by this enigmatic young lady, the Emperor decided to pay her a visit and so he travelled back with the bamboo cutter.

When they stepped inside his house, the Emperor saw Lady Kaguya. Her back was turned to him, and she was bathed in a wondrous glow. But when she turned and caught his gaze, she disappeared before his very eyes. The Emperor looked around bewildered and called her name, pleading with her to return.

And so she did.

At once the Emperor declared his undying love for this mysterious stranger, but Lady Kaguya explained once more, that if she left the house she would die. And so, with a heavy heart, the Emperor eventually left.

In time the Bamboo cutter and his wife noticed a change that gradually came over their daughter, she became quiet and pensive, and whenever she looked up at the full moon her eyes would fill with tears. At first she would not answer when asked if anything was wrong, but eventually, in an outpouring of grief, she explained that she was not of the Earth at all, but from the Moon, and that soon some of her fellow Moon People would come to take her back to the place of her birth.

Mystified, her father asked her why she had come to Earth. Lady Kaguya explained that there had been a great war on her world, and that she had been sent to Earth for her own safety. Now that the war was over, she would have to go home.

The Emperor soon heard this story, and fearing that he would lose her forever, he sent his personal guards to stop her from being taken away.

The guards waited for many days, and on the night of the next full Moon, a brilliant cloud descended from the heavens. It was so bright that the guards were almost blinded and rendered helpless. Within the cloud there were many Moon People, who descended from a strange craft. The Moon People approached the bamboo cutter's house, and ordered that Lady Kaguya return with them to their world.

Lady Kaguya knew there was no possibility of her staying on Earth, and so she stepped out of the house with her parents. A Moon Man handed her a bottle containing an Elixir of Immortality, and she took a deep gulp of the magical liquid. She apologized to her mother and father, and asked them to forgive her for causing them such pain.

She wrote a tearful message and handed it to the Emperor's most faithful guard, and asked that it, and the remains of the Elixir, be taken to the man who loved her more than anyone.

A Moon Man handed her a robe of feathers, which she put over her shoulders, and as she did so, all the sadness that had filled her heart disappeared – along with all her memories of the Earth, the Emperor and her parents. Then she ascended the steps into the craft, and set off with the other Moon People to their homeland.

The guard delivered the letter and the Elixir. The Emperor read how Lady Kaguya had wanted to be with him, that it pained her greatly to leave Earth, that their union was forbidden, and that she had to return to the Moon.

Upon finishing the letter, the Emperor was overcome with sadness. He turned to one of his courtiers and asked, "Which mountaintop is closest to heaven?"

He was told that it was a mountain in the Suruga Province. The Emperor handed the letter and Elixir to his most faithful guard, and asked him to take them to the top of the mountain and burn them both.

Upon seeing the stunned expressions of his courtiers, the Emperor explained that he did not want to drink the Elixir and become immortal, and remain forever with the thought that he would never see Lady Kaguya again.

So his men climbed to the top of the highest known mountain and carried out his orders. And to this day people still see smoke rising from the Mountain of Immortality, or Mount Fuji, and watch as the fumes become as one with the clouds of heaven.

The New Atlantis

Francis Bacon

Introduction

Francis Bacon (1561–1626) was an English philosopher, statesman, scientist and writer, whose works have had a profound influence across many spheres. As a politician he served as Attorney General and later as Lord Chancellor, while his scientific and philosophical works, not least *The New Atlantis*, influenced the formative years of The Royal Society.

The New Atlantis was first published in Latin as *Nova Atlantis* in 1624, and published in English in 1627. This unfinished utopian tale tells of a ship's crew who, after being blown off-course by violent winds, come across an uncharted island off South America. The travellers are amazed by the islanders' advanced ways, not least their scientific culture, and their advanced technologies which include the submarine, telescope, microscope, long-distance communication, flying machines and perpetual motion. The methods of reasoning that the islanders employ are, perhaps not surprisingly, based on Bacon's own scientific thought.

This tale is also unusual for its time, when Jews had been expelled from England, in showing Jews and Christians living harmoniously together.

The New Atlantis is one of a large number of utopian tales written in the sixteenth and seventeenth centuries. Other utopian stories written in this period include the early science fiction tales *The Man in the Moone* by Francis Godwin and *The Blazing World* by Margaret Cavendish.

For ease of reading, the spelling and punctuation in this version of tale have been modernized, and a glossary has been included at the end of the story. This glossary is well worth referencing first as the story contains many archaic and foreign-language words that may otherwise be confusing.

The New Atlantis

Francis Bacon

We sailed from Peru, where we had continued by the space of one whole year, for China and Japan, by the South Sea, taking with us victuals for twelve months, and had good winds from the east, though soft and weak, for five months' space and more. But then the wind came about, and settled in the west for many days, so as we could make little or no way, and were sometimes in purpose to turn back. But then again there arose strong and great winds from the south, with a point east, which carried us up, for all that we could do, toward the north, by which time our victuals failed us, though we had made good spare of them. So that finding ourselves, in the midst of the greatest wilderness of waters in the world, without victual, we gave ourselves for lost men, and prepared for death. Yet we did lift up our hearts and voices to God above, who showeth His wonders in the deep, beseeching Him of His mercy that as in the beginning He discovered the face of the deep, and brought forth dry land, so He would now discover land to us, that we might not perish.

And it came to pass that the next day about evening we saw within a kenning before us, towards the north, as it were thick clouds, which did put us in some hope

171

of land, knowing how that part of the South Sea was utterly unknown, and might have islands or continents that hitherto were not come to light. Wherefore we bent our course thither, where we saw the appearance of land, all that night, and in the dawning of next day we might plainly discern that it was a land flat to our sight, and full of boscage, which made it show the more dark. And after an hour and a half's sailing, we entered into a good haven, being the port of a fair city. Not great, indeed, but well built, and that gave a pleasant view from the sea. And we thinking every minute long till we were on land, came close to the shore and offered to land.

But straightway we saw divers of the people, with batons in their hands, as it were forbidding us to land, yet without any cries or fierceness, but only as warning us off, by signs that they made. Whereupon being not a little discomforted, we were advising with ourselves what we should do. During which time there made forth to us a small boat, with about eight persons in it, whereof one of them had in his hand a tipstaff of a yellow cane, tipped at both ends with blue, who made aboard our ship, without any show of distrust at all. And when he saw one of our number present himself somewhat afore the rest, he drew forth a little scroll of parchment (somewhat yellower than our parchment, and shining like the leaves of writing-tables, but otherwise soft and flexible) and delivered it to our foremost man. In which scroll were written in ancient Hebrew, and in ancient Greek, and in good Latin of the school, and in Spanish these words:

"Land ye not, none of you, and provide to be gone from this coast within sixteen days, except you have further time given you. Meanwhile, if you want fresh water, or victual, or help for your sick, or that your ship needeth repair, write down your wants, and you shall have that which belongeth to mercy."

This scroll was signed with a stamp of cherubim's wings, not spread, but hanging downward, and by them a cross.

This being delivered, the officer returned, and left only a servant with us to receive our answer. Consulting hereupon among ourselves, we were much perplexed. The denial of landing, and hasty warning us away, troubled us much. On the other side, to find that the people had languages, and were so full of humanity, did comfort us not a little. And above all, the sign of the cross to that instrument was to us a great rejoicing, and as it were a certain presage of good. Our answer was in the Spanish tongue: That for our ship, it was well, for we had rather met with calms and contrary winds, than any tempests. For our sick, they were many, and in very ill case, so that if they were not permitted to land, they ran in danger of their lives.

Our other wants we set down in particular, adding that we had some little store of merchandize, which if it pleased them to deal for, it might supply our wants, without being chargeable unto them. We offered some reward in pistoles unto the servant, and a piece of crimson velvet to be presented to the officer, but the servant took them not, nor would scarce look upon them, and so left us, and went back in another little boat which was sent for him.

About three hours after we had despatched our answer, there came toward us a person, as it seemed, of a place. He had on him a gown with wide sleeves, of a kind of water chamolet, of an excellent azure colour, far more glossy than ours. His under-apparel was green, and so was his hat, being in the form of a turban, daintily made, and not so huge as the Turkish turbans, and the locks of his hair came down below the brims of it. A reverend man was he to behold. He came in a boat, gilt in some part of it, with four persons more only in that boat, and was followed by another boat, wherein were some twenty. When he was come within a flight-shot of our ship, signs were made to us that we should send forth some to meet him upon the water, which we presently did in our ship-boat, sending the principal man amongst us save one, and four of our number with him.

When we were come within six yards of their boat, they called to us to stay, and not to approach farther, which we did. And thereupon the man, whom I before described, stood up, and with a loud voice in Spanish asked, "Are ye Christians?"

We answered, we were, fearing the less, because of the cross we had seen in the subscription. At which answer the said person lift up his right hand towards Heaven, and drew it softly to his mouth, which is the gesture they use, when they thank God, and then said: "If ye will swear, all of you, by the merits of the Saviour, that ye are no pirates, nor have shed blood lawfully or unlawfully, within forty days past, you may have license to come on land."

We said we were all ready to take that oath, whereupon one of those that were with him, being, as it seemed, a notary, made an entry of this act.

Which done, another of the attendants of the great person, which was with him in the same boat, after his lord had spoken a little to him, said aloud: "My lord would have you know that it is not of pride, or greatness, that he cometh not aboard your ship, but for that in your answer you declare that you have many sick amongst you, he was warned by the conservator of health of the city that he should keep a distance."

We bowed ourselves toward him and answered we were his humble servants, and accounted for great honour and singular humanity toward us, that which was already done, but hoped well that the nature of the sickness of our men was not infectious.

So he returned, and awhile after came the notary to us aboard our ship, holding in his hand a fruit of that country, like an orange, but of colour between orange-tawny and scarlet, which cast a most excellent odour. He used it, as it seemeth, for a preservative against infection. He gave us our oath, "By the name of Jesus, and His merits," and after told us that the next day, by six of the clock in the morning, we should be sent to, and brought to the strangers' house, so he called it, where we should be accommodated of things, both for our whole and for our sick.

So he left us, and when we offered him some pistoles, he smiling, said, "He must not be twice paid for one labour," meaning, as I take it, that he had salary sufficient of the State for his service. For, as I after learned, they call an officer that taketh rewards twice paid.

The next morning, early, there came to us the same officer that came to us at first, with his cane, and told us he came to conduct us to the strangers' house, and that he had prevented the hour, because we might have the whole day before us for our business.

"For," said he, "if you will follow my advice, there shall first go with me some few of you, and see the place, and how it may be made convenient for you, and then you may send for your sick, and the rest of your number which ye will bring on land."

We thanked him and said that his care which he took of desolate strangers, God would reward. And so six of us went on land with him, and when we were on land, he went before us, and turned to us and said he was but our servant and our guide. He led us through three fair streets, and all the way we went there were gathered some people on both sides, standing in a row, but in so civil a fashion, as if it had been, not to wonder at us, but to welcome us. And divers of them, as we passed by them, put their arms a little abroad, which is their gesture when they bid any welcome.

The strangers' house is a fair and spacious house, built of brick, of somewhat a bluer colour than our brick, and with handsome windows, some of glass, some of a kind of cambric oiled. He brought us first into a fair parlour above stairs, and then asked us what number of persons we were, and how many sick.

We answered, we were in all, sick and whole, one-and-fifty persons, whereof our sick were seventeen.

He desired us have patience a little, and to stay till he came back to us, which was about an hour after, and then he led us to see the chambers which were provided for us, being in number nineteen. They having cast it, as it seemeth, that four of those chambers, which were better than the rest, might receive four of the principal men of our company, and lodge them alone by themselves, and the other fifteen chambers were to lodge us, two and two together. The chambers were handsome and cheerful chambers, and furnished civilly. Then he led us to a long gallery, like a dorture, where he showed us all along the one side (for the other side was but wall and window) seventeen cells, very neat ones, having partitions of cedar wood. Which gallery and cells, being in all forty (many more than we needed) were instituted as an infirmary for sick persons. And he told us withal, that as any of our sick waxed well, he might be removed from his cell to a chamber, for which purpose there were set forth ten spare chambers, besides the number we spake of before.

This done, he brought us back to the parlour, and lifting up his cane a little, as they do when they give any charge or command, said to us: "Ye are to know that the custom of the land requireth that after this day and tomorrow, which we give you for removing your people from your ship, you are to keep within doors for three days. But let it not trouble you, nor do not think yourselves restrained, but rather left to your rest and ease. You shall want nothing, and there are six of our people appointed to attend you for any business you may have abroad."

He gave him thanks with all affection and respect, and said, "God surely is manifested in this land."

We offered him also twenty pistoles, but he smiled, and only said: "What? Twice paid!" And so he left us.

Soon after our dinner was served in, which was right good viands, both for bread and meat; better than any collegiate diet that I have known in Europe. We had also drink of three sorts, all wholesome and good: wine of the grape; a drink of grain, such as is with us our ale, but more clear; and a kind of cider made of a fruit of that country, a wonderful pleasing and refreshing drink. Besides, there were brought in to us great store of those scarlet oranges for our sick which, they said, were an assured remedy for sickness taken at sea. There was given us also a box of small gray or whitish pills, which they wished our sick should take, one of the pills every night before sleep which, they said, would hasten their recovery.

The next day, after that our trouble of carriage and removing of our men and goods out of our ship was somewhat settled and quiet, I thought good to call our company together and, when they were assembled, said unto them: "My dear friends, let us know ourselves, and how it standeth with us. We are men cast on land, as Jonas was out of the whale's belly, when we were as buried in the deep, and now we are on land, we are but between death and life, for we are beyond both the Old World and the New, and whether ever we shall see Europe, God only knoweth. It is a kind of miracle hath brought us hither, and it must be little less that shall bring us hence. Therefore in regard of our deliverance past, and our danger present and to come, let us look up to God, and every man reform his own ways. Besides, we are come here among a Christian people, full of piety and humanity. Let us not bring that confusion of face upon ourselves, as to show our vices or unworthiness before them. Yet there is more, for they have by commandment, though in form of courtesy, cloistered us within these walls for three days. Who knoweth whether it be not to take some taste of our manners and conditions? And if they find them bad, to banish us straightway, if good, to give us further time. For these men that they have given us for attendance, may withal have an eye upon us. Therefore, for God's love, and as we love the weal of our souls and bodies, let us so behave ourselves as we may be at peace with God and may find grace in the eyes of this people."

Our company with one voice thanked me for my good admonition, and promised me to live soberly and civilly, and without giving any the least occasion of offence. So we spent our three days joyfully, and without care, in expectation what would be done with us when they were expired. During which time, we had every hour joy of the amendment of our sick, who thought themselves cast into some divine pool of healing, they mended so kindly and so fast.

The morrow after our three days were past, there came to us a new man that we had not seen before, clothed in blue as the former was, save that his turban was white with a small red cross on top. He had also a tippet of fine linen. At his coming in, he did bend to us a little, and put his arms abroad. We of our parts saluted him in a very lowly and submissive manner, as looking that from him we should receive sentence of life or death. He desired to speak with some few of us. Whereupon six of us only stayed, and the rest avoided the room.

He said: "I am by office, governor of this house of strangers, and by vocation, I am a Christian priest, and therefore am come to you to offer you my service, both as strangers and chiefly as Christians. Some things I may tell you, which I think you will not be unwilling to hear. The State hath given you license to stay on land for the space of six weeks, and let it not trouble you if your occasions ask further time, for the law in this point is not precise, and I do not doubt but myself shall be able to obtain for you such further time as shall be convenient. Ye shall also understand that the strangers' house is at this time rich and much aforehand, for it hath laid up revenue these thirty-seven years, for so long it is since any stranger arrived in this part, and therefore take ye no care, the State will defray you all the time you stay. Neither shall you stay one day the less for that. As for any merchandize you have brought, ye shall be well used, and have your return, either in merchandize or in gold and silver, for to us it is all one. And if you have any other request to make, hide it not, for ye shall find we will not make your countenance to fall by the answer ye shall receive. Only this I must tell you, that none of you must go above a karan (that is with them a mile and a half) from the walls of the city, without special leave."

We answered, after we had looked awhile upon one another, admiring this gracious and parent-like usage, that we could not tell what to say, for we wanted words to express our thanks, and his noble free offers left us nothing to ask.

It seemed to us that we had before us a picture of our salvation in Heaven, for we that were awhile since in the jaws of death, were now brought into a place where we found nothing but consolations. For the commandment laid upon us, we would not fail to obey it, though it was impossible but our hearts should be inflamed to tread further upon this happy and holy ground. We added that our tongues should first cleave to the roofs of our mouths ere we should forget either this reverend person or this whole nation, in our prayers.

We also most humbly besought him to accept of us as his true servants, by as just a right as ever men on Earth were bounden, laying and presenting both our persons and all we had at his feet. He said he was a priest, and looked for a priest's reward, which was our brotherly love and the good of our souls and bodies. So he went from us, not without tears of tenderness in his eyes, and left us also confused with joy and kindness, saying among ourselves that we were come into a land of angels, which did appear to us daily, and prevent us with comforts, which we thought not of, much less expected.

The next day, about ten of the clock, the governor came to us again, and after salutations said familiarly that he was come to visit us, and called for a chair and sat him down. And we, being some ten of us (the rest were of the meaner sort or else gone abroad) sat down with him, and when we were sat he began thus: "We of this island of Bensalem (for so they called it in their language) have this: that by means of our solitary situation, and of the laws of secrecy, which we have for our travellers, and our rare admission of strangers, we know well most part of the habitable world, and are ourselves unknown. Therefore because he that knoweth least is fittest to ask questions it is more reason, for the entertainment of the time, that ye ask me questions, than that I ask you."

We answered, that we humbly thanked him that he would give us leave so to do. And that we conceived by the taste we had already, that there was no worldly thing on Earth more worthy to be known than the state of that happy land. But above all, we said, since that we were met from the several ends of the world, and hoped assuredly that we should meet one day in the kingdom of Heaven, for that we were both parts Christians, we desired to know, in respect that land was so remote, and so divided by vast and unknown seas from the land where our Saviour walked on Earth, who was the apostle of that nation, and how it was converted to the faith?

It appeared in his face that he took great contentment in this our question; he said: "Ye knit my heart to you by asking this question in the first place, for it showeth that you first seek the kingdom of Heaven, and I shall gladly, and briefly, satisfy your demand.

"About twenty years after the ascension of our Saviour, it came to pass that there was seen by the people of Renfusa, a city upon the eastern coast of our island, within night (the night was cloudy and calm) as it might be some mile in the sea, a great pillar of light; not sharp, but in form of a column, or cylinder, rising from the sea, a great way up towards Heaven, and on the top of it was seen a large cross of light, more bright and resplendent than the body of the pillar. Upon which so strange a spectacle, the people of the city gathered apace together upon the sands, to wonder, and so after put themselves into a number of small boats to go nearer to this marvellous sight. But when the boats were come within about sixty yards of the pillar, they found themselves all bound, and could go no further, yet so as they might move to go about, but might not approach nearer. So as the boats stood all as in a theater, beholding this light, as a Heavenly sign. It so fell out that there was in one of the boats one of the wise men of the Society of Salomon's House (which house, or college, my good brethren, is the very eye of this kingdom) who having awhile attentively and devoutly viewed and contemplated this pillar and cross, fell down upon his face, and then raised himself upon his knees, and lifting up his hands to Heaven, made his prayers in this manner:

"'Lord God of Heaven and Earth, thou hast vouchsafed of thy grace, to those of our order to know thy works of creation, and true secrets of them. And to discern, as far as appertaineth to the generations of men, between divine miracles, works of nature, works of art and impostures, and illusions of all sorts. I do here acknowledge and testify before this people that the thing we now see before our eyes is thy finger, and a true miracle. And forasmuch as we learn in our books that thou never workest miracles, but to a divine and excellent end, for the laws of nature are thine own laws, and thou exceedest them not but upon great cause, we most humbly beseech thee to prosper this great sign, and to give us the interpretation and use of it in mercy, which thou dost in some part secretly promise, by sending it unto us.'

"When he had made his prayer, he presently found the boat he was in movable and unbound, whereas all the rest remained still fast, and, taking that for an assurance of leave to approach, he caused the boat to be softly and with silence rowed toward the pillar. But ere he came near it, the pillar and cross of light broke up, and cast itself abroad, as it were, into a firmament of many stars, which also vanished soon after, and there was nothing left to be seen but a small ark or chest of cedar, dry and not wet at all with water, though it swam. And in the fore-end of it, which was toward him, grew a small green branch of palm, and when the wise man had taken it with all reverence into his boat, it opened of itself, and there were found in it a book and a letter, both written in fine parchment, and wrapped in sindons of linen. The book contained all the canonical books of the Old and New Testament, according as you have them, for we know well what the churches with you receive, and the Apocalypse itself, and some other books of the New Testament, which were not at that time written, were nevertheless in the book. And for the letter, it was in these words:

"'I, Bartholomew, a servant of the Highest, and apostle of Jesus Christ, was warned by an angel that appeared to me in a vision of glory, that I should commit this ark to the floods of the sea. Therefore I do testify and declare unto that people where God shall ordain this ark to come to land, that in the same day is come unto them salvation and peace, and good-will from the Father, and from the Lord Jesus.'

"There was also in both these writings, as well the book as the letter, wrought a great miracle, conform to that of the apostles, in the original gift of tongues. For there being at that time, in this land, Hebrews, Persians, and Indians, besides the natives, everyone read upon the book and letter, as if they had been written in his own language. And thus was this land saved from infidelity, as the remain of the old world was from water, by an ark, through the apostolical and miraculous evangelism of St. Bartholomew."

And here he paused, and a messenger came and called him forth from us. So this was all that passed in that conference.

The next day the same governor came again to us immediately after dinner and excused himself, saying that the day before he was called from us somewhat abruptly, but now he would make us amends, and spend time with us, if we held his company and

185

conference agreeable. We answered that we held it so agreeable and pleasing to us, as we forgot both dangers past, and fears to come, for the time we heard him speak, and that we thought an hour spent with him was worth years of our former life.

He bowed himself a little to us, and after we were set again, he said, "Well, the questions are on your part."

One of our number said, after a little pause, that there was a matter we were no less desirous to know than fearful to ask, lest we might presume too far. But, encouraged by his rare humanity toward us (that could scarce think ourselves strangers, being his vowed and professed servants) we would take the hardness to propound it, humbly beseeching him, if he thought it not fit to be answered, that he would pardon it, though he rejected it.

We said, we well observed those his words, which he formerly spake, that this happy island, where we now stood, was known to few, and yet knew most of the nations of the world, which we found to be true, considering they had the languages of Europe, and knew much of our State and business, and yet we in Europe, notwithstanding all the remote discoveries and navigations of this last age, never heard any of the least inkling or glimpse of this island. This we found wonderful strange; for that all nations have inter-knowledge one of another, either by voyage into foreign parts, or by strangers that come to them, and though the traveller into a foreign country doth commonly know more by the eye than he that stayeth at home can by relation of the traveller, yet both ways suffice to make a mutual knowledge, in some degree, on both parts. But for this island, we never heard tell of any ship of theirs that had been seen to arrive upon any shore of Europe, no, nor of either the East or West Indies, nor yet of any ship of any other part of the world, that had made return for them. And yet the marvel rested not in this. For the situation of it, as his lordship said, in the secret conclave of such a vast sea might cause it. But then, that they should have knowledge of the languages, books, affairs, of those that lie such a distance from them, it was a thing we could not tell what to make of, for that it seemed to us a condition and propriety of divine powers and beings, to be hidden and unseen to others, and yet to have others open, and as in a light to them.

At this speech the governor gave a gracious smile and said that we did well to ask pardon for this question we now asked, for that it imported, as if we thought this land a land of magicians, that sent forth spirits of the air into all parts, to bring them news and intelligence of other countries.

It was answered by us all, in all possible humbleness, but yet with a countenance taking knowledge, that we knew that he spake it but merrily. That we were apt enough to think there was somewhat supernatural in this island, but yet rather as angelical than magical. But to let his lordship know truly what it was that made us tender and doubtful to ask this question, it was not any such conceit, but because we remembered he had given a touch in his former speech, that this land had laws of secrecy touching strangers.

To this he said, "You remember it aright, and therefore in that I shall say to you, I must reserve some particulars, which it is not lawful for me to reveal, but there will be enough left to give you satisfaction. You shall understand, that which perhaps you will scarce think credible, that about three thousand years ago, or somewhat more, the navigation of the world, especially for remote voyages, was greater than at this day. Do not think with yourselves, that I know not how much it is increased with you, within these threescore years; I know it well, and yet I say, greater then than now. Whether it was, that the example of the ark, that saved the remnant of men from the universal deluge, gave men confidence to venture upon the waters, or what it was, but such is the truth. The Phoenicians, and especially the Tyrians, had great fleets, so had the Carthaginians their colony, which is yet farther west. Toward the east the shipping of Egypt, and of Palestine, was likewise great. China also, and the great Atlantis, that you call America, which have now but junks and canoes, abounded then in tall ships. This island, as appeareth by faithful registers of those times, had then fifteen hundred strong ships, of great content. Of all this there is with you sparing memory, or none, but we have large knowledge thereof.

"At that time this land was known and frequented by the ships and vessels of all the nations before named. And, as it cometh to pass, they had many times men of other countries, that were no sailors, that came with them, as Persians, Chaldeans, Arabians, so as almost all nations of might and fame resorted hither, of whom we have some stirps and little tribes with us at this day. And for our own ships, they went sundry voyages, as well to your straits, which you call the Pillars of Hercules, as to other parts in the Atlantic and Mediterranean seas, as to Paguin, which is the same with Cambalaine, and Quinzy, upon the Oriental seas, as far as to the borders of the East Tartary.

"At the same time, and an age after or more, the inhabitants of the great Atlantis did flourish. For though the narration and description which is made by a great man with you, that the descendants of Neptune planted there, and of the magnificent temple, palace, city, and hill, and the manifold streams of goodly navigable rivers, which as so many chains environed the same site and temple; and the several degrees of ascent, whereby men did climb up to the same, as if it had been a Scala Coeli, be all poetical and fabulous. Yet so much is true, that the said country of Atlantis, as well that of Peru, then called Coya, as that of Mexico, then named Tyrambel, were mighty and proud kingdoms, in arms, shipping, and riches; so mighty, as at one time, or at least within the space of ten years, they both made two great expeditions. They of Tyrambel through the Atlantic to the Mediterranean Sea, and they of Coya, through the South Sea upon this our island, and for the former of these, which was into Europe, the same author amongst you, as it seemeth, had some relation from the Egyptian priest, whom he citeth. For assuredly, such a thing there was. But whether it were the ancient Athenians that had the glory of the repulse and resistance of those forces, I can say nothing, but certain it is there never came back either ship or man from that voyage. Neither had the other voyage of those of Coya upon us had better fortune, if they had not met with enemies of greater clemency. For the King of this island, by name Altabin, a wise man and a great warrior, knowing well both his own strength and that of his enemies, handled the matter so as he cut off their land forces from their ships, and entoiled both their navy and their camp with a greater power than theirs, both by sea and land, and compelled them to render themselves without striking a stroke, and after they were at his mercy, contenting himself only with their oath, that they should no more bear arms against him, dismissed them all in safety.

"But the divine revenge overtook not long after those proud enterprises. For within less than the space of one hundred years, the Great Atlantis was utterly lost and destroyed; not by a great Earthquake, as your man saith, for that whole tract is little subject to Earthquakes, but by a particular deluge, or inundation; those countries having at this day far greater rivers, and far higher mountains to pour down waters, than any part of the old world. But it is true that the same inundation was not deep, nor past forty foot in most places, from the ground, so that although it destroyed man and beast generally, yet some few wild inhabitants of the wood escaped. Birds also were saved by flying to the high trees and woods. For as for men, although they had buildings in many places higher than the depth of the water, yet that inundation, though it were shallow, had a long continuance, whereby they of the vale that were not drowned perished for want of food, and other things necessary. So as marvel you not at the thin population of America, nor at the rudeness and ignorance of the people, for you must account your inhabitants of America as a young people, younger a thousand years at the least than the rest of the world, for that there was so much time between the universal flood and their particular inundation.

"For the poor remnant of human seed which remained in their mountains, peopled the country again slowly, by little and little, and being simple and a savage people (not like Noah and his sons, which was the chief family of the Earth) they were not able to leave letters, arts, and civility to their posterity. And having likewise in their mountainous habitations been used, in respect of the extreme cold of those regions, to clothe themselves with the skins of tigers, bears, and great hairy goats, that they have in those parts, when after they came down into the valley, and found the intolerable heats which are there, and knew no means of lighter apparel, they were forced to begin the custom of going naked, which continueth at this day. Only they take great pride and delight in the feathers of birds, and this also they took from those their ancestors of the mountains, who were invited unto it, by the infinite flight of birds, that came up to the high grounds, while the waters stood below. So you see, by this main accident of time, we lost our traffic with the

Americans, with whom of all others, in regard they lay nearest to us, we had most commerce. As for the other parts of the world, it is most manifest that in the ages following, whether it were in respect of wars, or by a natural revolution of time, navigation did everywhere greatly decay, and specially far voyages (the rather by the use of galleys, and such vessels as could hardly brook the ocean) were altogether left and omitted. So then, that part of intercourse which could be from other nations to sail to us, you see how it hath long since ceased, except it were by some rare accident, as this of yours. But now of the cessation of that other part of intercourse, which might be by our sailing to other nations, I must yield you some other cause. But I cannot say if I shall say truly, but our shipping, for number, strength, mariners, pilots, and all things that appertain to navigation, is as great as ever, and therefore why we should sit at home, I shall now give you an account by itself, and it will draw nearer, to give you satisfaction, to your principal question.

"There reigned in this land, about nineteen hundred years ago, a King, whose memory of all others we most adore; not superstitiously, but as a divine instrument, though a mortal man. His name was Salomon and we esteem him as the lawgiver of our nation. This King had a large heart, inscrutable for good, and was wholly bent to make his kingdom and people happy. He, therefore, taking into consideration how sufficient and substantive this land was, to maintain itself without any aid at all of the foreigner, being five thousand six hundred miles in circuit, and of rare fertility of soil, in the greatest part thereof. And finding also the shipping of this country might be plentifully set on work, both by fishing and by transportations from port to port, and likewise by sailing unto some small islands that are not far from us, and are under the crown and laws of this State. And recalling into his memory the happy and flourishing estate wherein this land then was, so as it might be a thousand ways altered to the worse, but scarce any one way to the better, though nothing wanted to his noble and heroical intentions, but only, as far as human foresight might reach, to give perpetuity to that which was in his time so happily established, therefore among his other fundamental laws of this kingdom he did ordain the interdicts and prohibitions which we have touching the entrance of strangers, which at that time, though it was after the calamity of America, was frequent, doubting novelties and commixture of manners. It is true, the like law against the admission of strangers without license is an ancient law in the Kingdom of China, and yet continued in use. But there it is a poor thing, and hath made them a curious, ignorant, fearful, foolish nation. But our lawgiver made his law of another temper. For first, he hath preserved all points of humanity, in taking order and making provision for the relief of strangers distressed, whereof you have tasted."

At which speech, as reason was, we all rose up and bowed ourselves.

He went on: "That King also still desiring to join humanity and policy together, and thinking it against humanity to detain strangers here against their wills, and against policy that they should return and discover their knowledge of this estate, he took this course: he did ordain, that of the strangers that should be permitted to land, as many at all times might depart as many as would, but as many as would stay, should have very good conditions, and means to live from the State. Wherein he saw so far, that now in so many ages since the prohibition, we have memory not of one ship that ever returned, and but of thirteen persons only, at several times, that chose to return in our bottoms. What those few that returned may have reported abroad, I know not. But you must think, whatsoever they have said, could be taken where they came but for a dream. Now for our travelling from hence into parts abroad, our lawgiver thought fit altogether to restrain it. So is it not in China. For the Chinese sail where they will, or can, which showeth, that their law of keeping out strangers is a law of pusillanimity and fear. But this restraint of ours hath one only exception, which is admirable; preserving the good which cometh by communicating with strangers, and avoiding the hurt, and I will now open it to you.

"And here I shall seem a little to digress, but you will by and by find it pertinent. Ye shall understand, my dear friends, that among the excellent acts of that King, one above all hath the pre-eminence. It was the erection and institution of an order, or society, which we call Salomon's House, the noblest foundation, as we think, that ever was upon the Earth, and the lantern of this kingdom. It is dedicated to the study of the works and creatures of God. Some think it beareth the founder's name a little corrupted, as if it should be Solomon's House. But the records write it as it is spoken. So as I take it to be denominate of the King of the Hebrews, which is famous with you, and no strangers to us, for we have some parts of his works which with you are lost, namely: that natural history which he wrote of all plants, from the cedar of Libanus to the moss that groweth out of the wall, and of all things that have life and motion. This maketh me think that our King finding himself to symbolize, in many things, with that King of the Hebrews, which lived many years before him, honoured him with the title of this foundation. And I am the rather induced to be of this opinion, for that I find in ancient records, this order or society is sometimes called Salomon's House, and sometimes the College of the Six Days' Works, whereby I am satisfied that our excellent King had learned from the Hebrews that God had created the world and all that therein is within six days. And therefore he instituted that house, for the finding out of the true nature of all things, whereby God might have the more glory in the workmanship of them, and men the more fruit in their use of them, did give it also that second name.

"But now to come to our present purpose. When the King had forbidden to all his people navigation into any part that was not under his crown, he made nevertheless this ordinance: that every twelve years there should be set forth out of this kingdom, two ships, appointed to several voyages; that in either of these ships there should be a mission of three of the fellows or brethren of Salomon's House, whose errand was only to give us knowledge of the affairs and state of those countries to which they were designed, and especially of the sciences, arts, manufactures, and inventions of all the world; and withal to bring unto us books, instruments, and patterns in every kind; that the ships, after they had landed the brethren, should return; and that the brethren should stay abroad till the new mission, the ships are not otherwise fraught than with store of victuals, and good quantity of treasure to remain with the brethren, for the buying of such things, and rewarding of such persons, as they should think fit.

Now for me to tell you how the vulgar sort of mariners are contained from being discovered at land, and how they must be put on shore for any time, colour themselves under the names of other nations, and to what places these voyages have been designed; and what places of rendezvous are appointed for the new missions, and the like circumstances of the practice, I may not do it, neither is it much to your desire. But thus you see we maintain a trade, not for gold, silver, or jewels, nor for silks, nor for spices, nor any other commodity of matter, but only for God's first creature, which was light, to have light, I say, of the growth of all parts of the world."

And when he had said this, he was silent, and so were we all, for indeed we were all astonished to hear so strange things so probably told. And he perceiving that we were willing to say somewhat, but had it not ready, in great courtesy took us off, and descended to ask us questions of our voyage and fortunes, and in the end concluded that we might do well to think with ourselves what time of stay we would demand of the State, and bade us not to scant ourselves, for he would procure such time as we desired. Whereupon we all rose up and presented ourselves to kiss the skirt of his tippet, but he would not suffer us, and so took his leave. But when it came once among our people that the State used to offer conditions to strangers that would stay, we had work enough to get any of our men to look to our ship, and to keep them from going presently to the governor to crave conditions, but with much ado we refrained them, till we might agree what course to take.

We took ourselves now for freemen, seeing there was no danger of our utter perdition, and lived most joyfully, going abroad and seeing what was to be seen in the city and places adjacent, within our tedder, and obtaining acquaintance with many of the city, not of the meanest quality, at whose hands we found such humanity, and such a freedom and desire to take strangers, as it were, into their bosom, as was enough to make us forget all that was dear to us in our own countries. And continually we met with many things, right worthy of observation and relation; as indeed, if there be a mirror in the world, worthy to hold men's eyes, it is that country.

One day there were two of our company bidden to a feast of the family, as they call it; a most natural, pious, and reverend custom it is, showing that nation to be compounded of all goodness. This is the manner of it: it is granted to any man that shall live to see thirty persons descended of his body, alive together, and all above three years old, to make this feast, which is done at the cost of the State. The father of the family, whom they call the tirsan, two days before the feast, taketh to him three of such friends as he liketh to choose, and is assisted also by the governor of the city or place where the feast is celebrated, and all the persons of the family, of both sexes, are summoned to attend him. These two days the tirsan sitteth in consultation, concerning the good estate of the family. There, if there be any discord or suits between any of the family, they are compounded and appeased. There, if any of the family be distressed or decayed, order is taken for their relief, and competent means to live. There, if any be subject to vice, or take ill-courses, they are reproved and censured. So, likewise, direction is given touching marriages, and the courses of life which any of them should take, with divers other the like orders and advices. The governor assisteth to the end, to put in execution, by his public authority, the decrees and orders of the tirsan, if they should be disobeyed, though that seldom needeth, such reverence and obedience they give to the order of nature.

The tirsan doth also then ever choose one man from among his sons, to live in house with him, who is called ever after the Son of the Vine. The reason will hereafter appear. On the feast day, the father, or tirsan, cometh forth after divine service into a large room where the feast is celebrated, which room hath a half-pace at the upper end. Against the wall, in the middle of the half-pace, is a chair placed for him, with a table and carpet before it. Over the chair is a state, made round or oval and it is of ivy; an ivy somewhat whiter than ours, like the leaf of a silver asp, but more shining, for it is green all winter. And the state is curiously wrought with silver and silk of divers colours, broiding or binding in the ivy, and is ever of the work of some of the daughters of the family, and veiled over at the top, with a fine net of silk and silver. But the substance of it is true ivy, whereof after it is taken down, the friends of the family are desirous to have some leaf or sprig to keep.

The tirsan cometh forth with all his generation or lineage, the males before him, and the females following him, and if there be a mother, from whose body the whole lineage is descended, there is a traverse placed in a loft above on the right hand of the chair, with a privy door, and a carved window of glass, leaded with gold and blue, where she sitteth, but is not seen.

When the tirsan is come forth, he sitteth down in the chair, and all the lineage place themselves against the wall, both at his back, and upon the return of the half-pace, in order of their years, without difference of sex, and stand upon their feet. When he is set, the room being always full of company, but well-kept and without disorder, after some pause there cometh in from the lower end of the room a taratan (which is as much as a herald) and on either side of him two young lads, whereof one carrieth a scroll of their shining yellow parchment, and the other a cluster of grapes of gold, with a long foot or stalk. The herald and children are clothed with mantles of sea-water green satin, but the herald's mantle is streamed with gold, and hath a train. Then the herald with three courtesies, or rather inclinations, cometh up as far as the half-pace, and there first taketh into his hand the scroll. This scroll is the King's charter, containing gift of revenue, and many privileges, exemptions, and points of honour, granted to the father of the family, and it is ever styled and directed, "To such an one, our well-beloved friend and creditor," which is a title proper only to this case. For they say, the King is debtor to no man, but for propagation of his subjects.

The seal set to the King's charter is the King's image, embossed or moulded in gold, and though such charters be expedited of course, and as of right, yet they are varied by discretion, according to the number and dignity of the family. This charter the herald readeth aloud, and while it is read, the father, or tirsan, standeth up, supported by two of his sons, such as he chooseth. Then the herald mounteth the half-pace, and delivereth the charter into his hand; and with that there is an acclamation, by all that are present, in their language, which is thus much, "Happy are the people of Bensalem." Then the herald taketh into his hand from the other child the cluster of grapes, which is of gold; both the stalk, and the grapes. But the grapes are daintily enamelled, and if the males of the family be the greater number, the grapes are enamelled purple, with a little sun set on the top; if the females, then they are enamelled into a greenish yellow, with a crescent on the top. The grapes are in number as many as there are descendants of the family. This golden cluster the herald delivereth also to the tirsan, who presently delivereth it over to that son that he had formerly chosen, to be in house with him, who beareth it before his father, as an ensign of honour, when he goeth in public ever after, and is thereupon called the Son of the Vine.

After this ceremony ended the father, or tirsan, retireth, and after some time cometh forth again to dinner, where he sitteth alone under the state, as before, and none of his descendants sit with him, of what degree or dignity so ever, except he hap to be of Salomon's House.

He is served only by his own children, such as are male, who perform unto him all service of the table upon the knee, and the women only stand about him, leaning against the wall. The room below his half-pace hath tables on the sides for the guests that are bidden, who are served with great and comely order, and toward the end of dinner (which in the greatest feasts with them lasteth never above an hour and a half) there is a hymn sung, varied according to the invention of him that composeth it (for they have excellent poesy) but the subject of it is always the praises of Adam, and Noah, and Abraham, whereof the former two peopled the world, and the last was the father of the faithful, concluding ever with a thanksgiving for the nativity of our Saviour, in whose birth the births of all are only blessed.

Dinner being done, the tirsan retireth again, and having withdrawn himself alone into a place, where he maketh some private prayers, he cometh forth the third time, to give the blessing, with all his descendants, who stand about him as at the first. Then he calleth them forth by one and by one, by name as he pleaseth, though seldom the order of age be inverted. The person that is called (the table being before removed) kneeleth down before the chair, and the father layeth his hand upon his head, or her head, and giveth the blessing in these words: "Son of Bensalem (or daughter of Bensalem), thy father saith it; the man by whom thou hast breath and life speaketh the word; the blessing of the everlasting Father, the Prince of Peace, and the Holy Dove be upon thee, and make the days of thy pilgrimage good and many." This he saith to every of them, and that done, if there be any of his sons of eminent merit and virtue, so they be not above two, he calleth for them again, and saith, laying his arm over their shoulders, they standing: "Sons, it is well you are born, give God the praise, and persevere to the end." And withal delivereth to either of them a jewel, made in the figure of an ear of wheat, which they ever after wear in the front of their turban, or hat. This done, they fall to music and dances, and other recreations, after their manner, for the rest of the day. This is the full order of that feast.

By that time six or seven days were spent, I was fallen into straight acquaintance with a merchant of that city, whose name was Joabin. He was a Jew and circumcised, for they have some few stirps of Jews yet remaining among them, whom they leave to their own religion. Which they may the better do, because they are of a far differing disposition from the Jews in other parts. For whereas they hate the name of Christ, and have a secret inbred rancour against the people among whom they live, these, contrariwise, give unto our Saviour many high attributes, and love the nation of Bensalem extremely. Surely this man of whom I speak would ever acknowledge that Christ was born of a Virgin, and that he was more than a man, and he would tell how God made him ruler of the seraphim, which guard his throne, and they call him also the Milken Way, and the Eliah of the Messiah, and many other high names, which though they be inferior to his divine majesty, yet they are far from the language of other Jews. And for the country of Bensalem, this man would make no end of commending it, being desirous by tradition among the Jews there to have it believed that the people thereof were of the generations of Abraham, by another son, whom they call Nachoran, and that Moses by a secret cabala ordained the laws of Bensalem which they now use, and that when the Messias should come, and sit in his throne at Hierusalem, the King of Bensalem should sit at his feet, whereas other kings should keep a great distance. But yet setting aside these Jewish dreams, the man was a wise man and learned, and of great policy, and excellently seen in the laws and customs of that nation.

Among other discourses one day I told him, I was much affected with the relation I had from some of the company of their custom in holding the feast of the family, for that, methought, I had never heard of a solemnity wherein nature did so much preside. And because propagation of families proceedeth from the nuptial copulation, I desired to know of him what laws and customs they had concerning marriage, and whether they kept marriage well, and whether they were tied to one wife? For that where population is so much affected, and such as with them it seemed to be, there is commonly permission of plurality of wives.

To this he said: "You have reason for to commend that excellent institution of the feast of the family, and indeed we have experience, that those families that are partakers of the blessings of that feast, do flourish and prosper ever after, in an extraordinary manner. But hear me now, and I will tell you what I know. You shall understand that there is not under the Heavens so chaste a nation as this of Bensalem, nor so free from all pollution or foulness. It is the virgin of the world. I remember, I have read in one of your European books, of a holy hermit among you, that desired to see the spirit of fornication, and there appeared to him a little foul ugly Ethiope, but if he had desired to see the spirit of chastity of Bensalem, it would have appeared to him in the likeness of a fair beautiful cherub, for there is nothing, among mortal men, more fair and admirable than the chaste minds of this people.

"Know, therefore, that with them there are no stews, no dissolute houses, no courtesans, nor anything of that kind. Nay, they wonder, with detestation, at you in Europe, which permit such things. They say ye have put marriage out of office, for marriage is ordained a remedy for unlawful concupiscence, and natural concupiscence seemeth as a spur to marriage. But when men have at hand a remedy, more agreeable to their corrupt will, marriage is almost expulsed. And therefore there are with you seen infinite men that marry not, but choose rather a libertine and impure single life, than to be yoked in marriage, and many that do marry, marry late, when the prime and strength of their years are past. And when they do marry, what is marriage to them but a very bargain, wherein is sought alliance, or portion, or reputation, with some desire (almost indifferent) of issue, and not the faithful nuptial union of man and wife, that was first instituted. Neither is it possible that those that have cast away so basely so much of their strength, should greatly esteem children (being of the same matter) as chaste men do. So likewise during marriage is the case much amended, as it ought to be if those things were tolerated only for necessity; no, but they remain still as a very affront to marriage.

"The haunting of those dissolute places, or resort to courtesans, are no more punished in married men than in bachelors. And the depraved custom of change, and the delight in meretricious embracements, where sin is turned into art, maketh marriage a dull thing, and a kind of imposition or tax. They hear you defend these things, as done to avoid greater evils, as advoutries, deflowering of virgins, unnatural lust, and the like. But they say this is a preposterous wisdom, and they call it Lot's offer, who to save his guests from abusing, offered his daughters, nay, they say further, that there is little gained in this, for that the same vices and appetites do still remain and abound, unlawful lust being like a furnace, that if you stop the flames altogether it will quench, but if you give it any vent it will rage. As for masculine love, they have no touch of it, and yet there are not so faithful and inviolate friendships in the world again as are there, and to speak generally, as I said before, I have not read of any such chastity in any people as theirs. And their usual saying is that whosoever is unchaste cannot reverence himself, and they say that the reverence of a man's self, is, next to religion, the chiefest bridle of all vices."

And when he had said this, the good Jew paused a little, whereupon I, far more willing to hear him speak on than to speak myself, yet thinking it decent that upon his pause of speech I should not be altogether silent, said only this: that I would say to him, as the widow of Sarepta said to Elias, that he was come to bring to memory our sins, and that I confess the righteousness of Bensalem was greater than the righteousness of Europe. At which speech he bowed his head, and went on this manner:

"They have also many wise and excellent laws, touching marriage. They allow no polygamy. They have ordained that none do intermarry, or contract, until a month be past from their first interview. Marriage without consent of parents they do not make void, but they mulct it in the inheritors, for the children of such marriages are not admitted to inherit above a third part of their parents' inheritance. I have read in a book of one of your men, of a feigned commonwealth, where the married couple are permitted, before they contract, to see one another naked. This they dislike, for they think it a scorn to give a refusal after so familiar knowledge, but because of many hidden defects in men and women's bodies, they have a more civil way, for they have near every town a couple of pools, which they call Adam and Eve's pools, where it is permitted to one of the friends of the man, and another of the friends of the woman, to see them severally bathe naked."

And as we were thus in conference, there came one that seemed to be a messenger, in a rich huke, that spake with the Jew, whereupon he turned to me, and said, "You will pardon me, for I am commanded away in haste."

The next morning he came to me again, joyful as it seemed, and said: "There is word come to the governor of the city, that one of the fathers of Salomon's House will be here this day seven-night. We have seen none of them this dozen years. His coming is in state, but the cause of this coming is secret. I will provide you and your fellows of a good standing to see his entry."

I thanked him, and told him I was most glad of the news.

The day being come he made his entry. He was a man of middle stature and age, comely of person, and had an aspect as if he pitied men. He was clothed in a robe of fine black cloth and wide sleeves, and a cape. His under-garment was of excellent white linen down to the foot, girt with a girdle of the same, and a sindon or tippet of the same about his neck. He had gloves that were curious, and set with stone, and shoes of peach-coloured velvet. His neck was bare to the shoulders. His hat was like a helmet, or Spanish montero, and his locks curled below it decently; they were of colour brown. His beard was cut round and of the same colour with his hair, somewhat lighter. He was carried in a rich chariot, without wheels, litter-wise, with two horses at either end, richly trapped in blue velvet embroidered, and two footmen on each side in the like attire. The chariot was all of cedar, gilt and adorned with crystal, save that the fore end had panels of sapphires set in borders of gold, and the hinder end the like of emeralds of the Peru colour. There was also a sun of gold, radiant upon the top, in the midst, and on the top before a small cherub of gold, with wings displayed. The chariot was covered with cloth-of-gold tissued upon blue.

He had before him fifty attendants, young men all, in white satin loose coats up to the mid-leg, and stockings of white silk, and shoes of blue velvet, and hats of blue velvet, with fine plumes of divers colours, set round like hat-bands. Next before the chariot went two men, bareheaded, in linen garments down to the foot, girt, and shoes of blue velvet, who carried the one a crosier, the other a pastoral staff like a sheep-hook; neither of them of metal, but the crosier of balm-wood, the pastoral staff of cedar. Horsemen he had none, neither before nor behind his chariot, as it seemeth, to avoid all tumult and trouble. Behind his chariot went all the officers and principals of the companies of the city. He sat alone, upon cushions, of a kind of excellent plush, blue, and under his foot curious carpets of silk of divers colours, like the Persian, but far finer. He held up his bare hand, as he went, as blessing the people, but in silence. The street was wonderfully well kept, so that there was never any army had their men stand in better battle-array than the people stood. The windows likewise were not crowded, but everyone stood in them, as if they had been placed.

When the show was passed, the Jew said to me, "I shall not be able to attend you as I would, in regard of some charge the city hath laid upon me for the entertaining of this great person."

Three days after the Jew came to me again, and said: "Ye are happy men, for the father of Salomon's House taketh knowledge of your being here, and commanded me to tell you that he will admit all your company to his presence, and have private conference with one of you, that ye shall choose, and for this hath appointed the next day after tomorrow. And because he meaneth to give you his blessing, he hath appointed it in the forenoon."

We came at our day and hour, and I was chosen by my fellows for the private access. We found him in a fair chamber, richly hanged, and carpeted under foot, without any degrees to the state. He was sat upon a low throne richly adorned, and a rich cloth of state over his head of blue satin embroidered. He was alone, save that he had two pages of honour, on either hand one, finely attired in white. His undergarments were the like that we saw him wear in the chariot, but instead of his gown, he had on him a mantle with a cape, of the same fine black, fastened about him. When we came in, as we were taught, we bowed low at our first entrance, and when we were come near his chair, he stood up, holding forth his hand un-gloved, and in posture of blessing, and we every one of us stooped down and kissed the hem of his tippet. That done, the rest departed, and I remained. Then he warned the pages forth of the room, and caused me to sit down beside him, and spake to me thus in the Spanish tongue:

"God bless thee, my son. I will give thee the greatest jewel I have. For I will impart unto thee, for the love of God and men, a relation of the true state of Salomon's House. Son, to make you know the true state of Salomon's House, I will keep this order. First, I will set forth unto you the end of our foundation. Secondly, the preparations and instruments we have for our works. Thirdly, the several employments and functions whereto our fellows are assigned. And fourthly, the ordinances and rites which we observe.

"The end of our foundation is the knowledge of causes, and secret motions of things, and the enlarging of the bounds of human empire, to the effecting of all things possible.

"The preparations and instruments are these: We have large and deep caves of several depths. The deepest are sunk six hundred fathoms, and some of them are digged and made under great hills and mountains so that if you reckon together the depth of the hill and the depth of the cave, they are, some of them, above three miles deep. For we find that the depth of a hill and the depth of a cave from the flat are the same thing; both remote alike from the sun and Heaven's beams, and from the open air. These caves we call the lower region. And we use them for all coagulations, indurations, refrigerations, and conservations of bodies. We use them likewise for the imitation of natural mines and the producing also of new artificial metals, by compositions and materials which we use and lay there for many years. We use them also sometimes, which may seem strange, for curing of some diseases, and for prolongation of life, in some hermits that choose to live there, well accommodated of all things necessary, and indeed live very long, by whom also we learn many things.

"We have burials in several earths, where we put divers cements, as the Chinese do their porcelain. But we have them in greater variety, and some of them more fine. We also have great variety of composts and soils, for the making of the earth fruitful.

"We have high towers, the highest about half a mile in height, and some of them likewise set upon high mountains, so that the vantage of the hill with the tower is in the highest of them three miles at least. And these places we call the upper region, account the air between the high places and the low as a middle region. We use these towers, according to their several heights and situations, for insulation, refrigeration, conservation, and for the view of divers meteors, as winds, rain, snow, hail, and some of the fiery meteors also. And upon them in some places are dwellings of hermits, whom we visit sometimes and instruct what to observe.

"We have great lakes, both salt and fresh, whereof we have use for the fish and fowl. We use them also for burials of some natural bodies, for we find a difference in things buried in earth, or in air below the earth, and things buried in water. We have also pools, of which some do strain fresh water out of salt, and others by art do turn fresh water into salt. We have also some rocks in the midst of the sea, and some bays upon the shore for some works, wherein are required the air and vapour of the sea. We have likewise violent streams and cataracts, which serve us for many motions, and likewise engines for multiplying and enforcing of winds to set also on divers motions.

"We have also a number of artificial wells and fountains, made in imitation of the natural sources and baths, as tincted upon vitriol, sulphur, steel, brass, lead, nitre, and other minerals, and again, we have little wells for infusions of many things, where the waters take the virtue quicker and better than in vessels or basins. And among them we have a water, which we call water of paradise, being by that we do it made very sovereign for health and prolongation of life.

"We have also great and spacious houses, where we imitate and demonstrate meteors, as snow, hail, rain, some artificial rains of bodies and not of water, thunders, lightnings; also generations of bodies in air, as frogs, flies, and divers others.

"We have also certain chambers, which we call chambers of health, where we qualify the air as we think good and proper for the cure of divers diseases and preservation of health.

"We have also fair and large baths, of several mixtures, for the cure of diseases, and the restoring of man's body from arefaction, and others for the confirming of it in strength of sinews, vital parts, and the very juice and substance of the body.

"We have also large and various orchards and gardens, wherein we do not so much respect beauty as variety of ground and soil, proper for divers trees and herbs, and some very spacious, where trees and berries are set, whereof we make divers kinds of drinks, beside the vineyards. In these we practise likewise all conclusions of grafting, and inoculating, as well of wild-trees as fruit-trees, which produceth many effects. And we make by art, in the same orchards and gardens, trees and flowers, to come earlier or later than their seasons, and to come up and bear more speedily than by their natural course they do. We make them also by art greater much than their nature, and their fruit greater and sweeter, and of differing taste, smell, colour, and figure, from their nature. And many of them we so order as that they become of medicinal use.

"We have also means to make divers plants rise by mixtures of earths without seeds, and likewise to make divers new plants, differing from the vulgar, and to make one tree or plant turn into another.

"We have also parks, and enclosures of all sorts, of

beasts and birds, which we use not only for view or rareness, but likewise for dissections and trials, that thereby we may take light what may be wrought upon the body of man. Wherein we find many strange effects, as continuing life in them, though divers parts, which you account vital, be perished and taken forth, resuscitating of some that seem dead in appearance, and the like. We try also all poisons, and other medicines upon them, as well of chirurgery as physic. By art likewise we make them greater or taller than their kind is, and contrariwise dwarf them and stay their growth, we make them more fruitful and bearing than their kind is, and contrariwise barren and not generative. Also we make them differ in colour, shape, activity, many ways. We find means to make commixtures and copulations of divers kinds, which have produced many new kinds, and them not barren, as the general opinion is. We make a number of kinds of serpents, worms, flies, fishes of putrefaction, whereof some are advanced, in effect, to be perfect creatures, like beasts or birds, and have sexes, and do propagate. Neither do we this by chance, but we know beforehand of what matter and commixture, what kind of those creatures will arise.

"We have also particular pools where we make trials upon fishes, as we have said before of beasts and birds.

"We have also places for breed and generation of those kinds of worms and flies which are of special use, such as are with you your silkworms and bees.

"I will not hold you long with recounting of our

brew-houses, bake-houses, and kitchens, where are made divers drinks, breads, and meats, rare and of special effects. Wines we have of grapes, and drinks of other juice, of fruits, of grains, and of roots, and of mixtures with honey, sugar, manna, and fruits dried and decocted; also of the tears or wounding of trees and of the pulp of canes. And these drinks are of several ages, some to the age or last of forty years. We have drinks also brewed with several herbs and roots and spices, yea, with several fleshes and white meats, whereof some of the drinks are such as they are in effect meat and drink both, so that divers, especially in age, do desire to live with them with little or no meat or bread. And above all we strive to have drinks of extreme thin parts, to insinuate into the body, and yet without all biting, sharpness, or fretting; insomuch as some of them put upon the back of your hand, will with a little stay pass through to the palm, and yet taste mild to the mouth. We have also waters, which we ripen in that fashion, as they become nourishing, so that they are indeed excellent drinks, and many will use no other. Bread we have of several grains, roots, and kernels, yea, and some of flesh, and fish, dried, with divers kinds of leavings and seasonings, so that some do extremely move appetites, some do nourish so as divers do live of them, without any other meat, who live very long. So for meats, we have some of them so beaten, and made tender, and mortified, yet without all corrupting, as a weak heat of the stomach will turn them into good chilus, as well as a strong heat would meat otherwise prepared. We have some meats also and bread, and drinks, which, taken by men, enable them to fast long after, and some other, that used make the very flesh of men's bodies sensibly more hard and tough, and their strength far greater than otherwise it would be.

"We have dispensatories or shops of medicines, wherein you may easily think, if we have such variety of plants, and living creatures, more than you have in Europe, for we know what you have, the simples, drugs, and ingredients of medicines, must likewise be in so much the greater variety. We have them likewise of divers ages, and long fermentations. And for their preparations, we have not only all manner of exquisite distillations, and separations, and especially by gentle heats, and percolations through divers strainers, yea, and substances, but also exact forms of composition, whereby they incorporate almost as they were natural simples.

"We have also divers mechanical arts, which you have not, and stuffs made by them, as papers, linen, silks, tissues, dainty works of feathers of wonderful lustre, excellent dyes, and many others, and shops likewise as well for such as are not brought into vulgar use among us, as for those that are. For you must know, that of the things before recited, many of them are grown into use throughout the kingdom, but yet, if they did flow from our invention, we have of them also for patterns and principals.

"We have also furnaces of great diversities, and that keep great diversity of heats, fierce and quick, strong and constant, soft and mild, blown, quiet, dry, moist, and the like. But above all we have heats, in imitation of the Sun's and Heavenly bodies' heats, that pass divers inequalities, and as it were orbs, progresses, and returns whereby we produce admirable effects. Besides, we have heats of dungs, and of bellies and maws of living creatures and of their bloods and bodies, and of hays and herbs laid up moist, of lime unquenched, and such like. Instruments also which generate heat only by motion. And farther, places for strong insulations, and, again, places under the earth, which by nature or art yield heat. These divers heats we use as the nature of the operation which we intend requireth.

"We have also perspective houses, where we make demonstrations of all lights and radiations and of all colours; and out of things uncoloured and transparent we can represent unto you all several colours, not in rainbows, as it is in gems and prisms, but of themselves single. We represent also all multiplications of light, which we carry to great distance, and make so sharp as to discern small points and lines. Also: all colourations of light; all delusions and deceits of the sight, in figures, magnitudes, motions, colours; all demonstrations of shadows. We find also divers means, yet unknown to you, of producing of light, originally from divers bodies. We procure means of seeing objects afar off, as in the Heaven and remote places, and represent things near as afar off, and things afar off as near, making feigned distances. We have also helps for the sight far above spectacles and glasses in use. We have also glasses and means to see small and minute bodies, perfectly and distinctly, as the shapes and colours of small flies and worms, grains, and flaws in gems which cannot otherwise be seen, observations in urine and blood not otherwise to be seen. We make artificial rainbows, halos, and circles about light. We represent also all manner of reflections, refractions, and multiplications of visual beams of objects.

"We have also precious stones, of all kinds, many of them of great beauty and to you unknown, crystals likewise, and glasses of divers kind, and among them some of metals vitrificated, and other materials, besides those of which you make glass. Also a number of fossils and imperfect minerals, which you have not. Likewise loadstones of prodigious virtue, and other rare stones, both natural and artificial.

"We have also sound-houses, where we practise and demonstrate all sounds and their generation. We have harmony which you have not, of quarter-sounds and lesser slides of sounds. Divers instruments of music likewise to you unknown, some sweeter than any you have, together with bells and rings that are dainty and sweet. We represent small sounds as great and deep, likewise great sounds extenuate and sharp, we make divers tremblings and warblings of sounds, which in their original are entire. We represent and imitate all articulate sounds and letters, and the voices and notes of beasts and birds. We have certain helps which, set to the ear, do further the hearing greatly, we have also divers strange and artificial echoes, reflecting the voice many times, and, as it were, tossing it, and some that give back the voice louder than it came, some shriller and some deeper, yea, some rendering the voice, differing in the letters or articulate sound from that they receive. We have all means to convey sounds in trunks and pipes, in strange lines and distances.

"We have also perfume-houses, wherewith we join also practices of taste. We multiply smells which may seem strange, we imitate smells, making all smells to breathe out of other mixtures than those that give them. We make divers imitations of taste likewise, so that they will deceive any man's taste. And in this house we contain also a confiture-house, where we make all sweetmeats, dry and moist, and divers pleasant wines, milks, broths, and salads, far in greater variety than you have.

"We have also engine-houses, where are prepared engines and instruments for all sorts of motions. There we imitate and practise to make swifter motions than any you have, either out of your muskets or any engine that you have, and to make them and multiply them more easily and with small force, by wheels and other means, and to make them stronger and more violent than yours are, exceeding your greatest cannons and basilisks. We represent also ordnance and instruments of war and engines of all kinds, and likewise new mixtures and compositions of gunpowder, wild-fires burning in water and unquenchable, also fireworks of all variety, both for pleasure and use. We imitate also flights of birds; we have some degrees of flying in the air. We have ships and boats for going under water and brooking of seas, also swimming-girdles and supporters. We have divers curious clocks and other like motions of return, and some perpetual motions. We imitate also motions of living creatures by images of men, beasts, birds, fishes, and serpents; we have also a great number of other various motions, strange for equality, fineness, and subtlety.

"We have also a mathematical-house, where are represented all instruments, as well of geometry as astronomy, exquisitely made.

"We have also houses of deceits of the senses, where we represent all manner of feats of juggling, false apparitions, impostures and illusions, and their fallacies. And surely you will easily believe that we, that have so many things truly natural which induce admiration, could in a world of particulars deceive the senses if we would disguise those things, and labour to make them seem more miraculous. But we do hate all impostures and lies, insomuch as we have severely forbidden it to all our fellows, under pain of ignominy and fines, that they do not show any natural work or thing adorned or swelling, but only pure as it is, and without all affectation of strangeness.

"These are, my son, the riches of Salomon's House.

"For the several employments and offices of our fellows, we have twelve that sail into foreign countries under the names of other nations (for our own we conceal), who bring us the books and abstracts, and patterns of experiments of all other parts. These we call merchants of light.

"We have three that collect the experiments which are in all books. These we call depredators.

"We have three that collect the experiments of all mechanical arts, and also of liberal sciences, and also of practices which are not brought into arts. These we call mystery-men.

"We have three that try new experiments, such as themselves think good. These we call pioneers or miners.

"We have three that draw the experiments of the former four into titles and tables, to give the better light for the drawing of observations and axioms out of them. These we call compilers. We have three that bend themselves, looking into the experiments of their fellows, and cast about how to draw out of them things of use and practice for man's life and knowledge, as well for works as for plain demonstration of causes, means of natural divinations, and the easy and clear discovery of the virtues and parts of bodies. These we call dowry-men or benefactors.

"Then after divers meetings and consults of our whole number, to consider of the former labours and collections, we have three that take care out of them to direct new experiments, of a higher light, more penetrating into nature than the former. These we call lamps.

"We have three others that do execute the experiments so directed, and report them. These we call inoculators.

"Lastly, we have three that raise the former discoveries by experiments into greater observations, axioms, and aphorisms. These we call interpreters of nature.

"We have also, as you must think, novices and apprentices, that the succession of the former employed men do not fail, besides a great number of servants and attendants, men and women. And this we do also: we have consultations, which of the inventions and experiences which we have discovered shall be published, and which not, and take all an oath of secrecy for the concealing of those which we think fit to keep secret, though some of those we do reveal sometime to the State, and some not.

"For our ordinances and rites we have two very long and fair galleries. In one of these we place patterns and samples of all manner of the more rare and excellent inventions, in the other we place the statues of all principal inventors. There we have the statue of your Columbus, that discovered the West Indies, also the inventor of ships, your monk that was the inventor of ordnance and of gunpowder, the inventor of music, the inventor of letters, the inventor of printing, the inventor of observations of astronomy, the inventor of works in metal, the inventor of glass, the inventor of silk of the worm, the inventor of wine, the inventor of corn and bread, the inventor of sugars; and all these by more certain tradition than you have. Then we have divers inventors of our own, of excellent works, which, since you have not seen, it were too long to make descriptions of them, and besides, in the right understanding of those descriptions you might easily err. For upon every invention of value we erect a statue to the inventor, and give him a liberal and honourable reward. These statues are some of brass, some of marble and touchstone, some of cedar and other special woods gilt and adorned; some of iron, some of silver, some of gold.

"We have certain hymns and services, which we say daily, of laud and thanks to God for His marvellous works. And forms of prayers, imploring His aid and blessing for the illumination of our labours, and turning them into good and holy uses.

"Lastly, we have circuits or visits, of divers principal cities of the kingdom, where as it cometh to pass we do publish such new profitable inventions as we think good. And we do also declare natural divinations of diseases, plagues, swarms of hurtful creatures, scarcity, tempests, earthquakes, great inundations, comets, temperature of the year, and divers other things, and we give counsel thereupon, what the people shall do for the prevention and remedy of them."

And when he had said this he stood up, and I, as I had been taught, knelt down, and he laid his right hand upon my head, and said:

"God bless thee, my son, and God bless this relation which I have made. I give thee leave to publish it, for the good of other nations, for we here are in God's bosom, a land unknown."

And so he left me, having assigned a value of about two thousand ducats for a bounty to me and my fellows, for they give great largesses, where they come, upon all occasions.

Glossary

Advoutries Adultery

Appertaineth Pertain

Arefaction Drying

Bidden Invited

Boscage Wood or thicket

Boundon Obliged or bound to do something

Broiding Braiding

Cambric A thin plain fabric

Chirurgery Surgery

Coagulation Clot

Concupiscence Strong desire or lust

Crosier Religious ceremonial staff

Decoct Extract an essence by boiling

Dorture Dormitory

Ducat A gold coin

Girt Surrounded

Half-Pace A broad step or small landing between two half-flights in a staircase

Huke An outer garment

Impostures Deception or imposter

Induration Hardening

Largess Money or gifts

Kenning Maximum distance visible from sea (approximately twenty miles)

Meretricious Based on deception

Mulct Extort

Morrow Morning

Pillars of Hercules Strait of Gibraltar

Pistole A Spanish coin

Poesy Poem or poetic skill

Pusillanimity Cowardliness

Simples Chemicals of only one substance

Sindons Cloth, usually of silk or linen

Space Duration

Stirps Descendants

Tincted Imbued

Tippet Neck garment

Tipstaff Staff carried by an official

Touchstone A black stone rich in silica

Viands Food

Vitrificated Converted into glass

Weal Well being

We hope you enjoyed reading The New Atlantis and Other Early Science Fiction Tales. Firestone Books also has two Early Science Fiction anthologies as well as separate eBooks, showing the wealth of science fiction that was around before Verne, Wells and other science fiction pioneers.

Out paperbacks include:

Early Science Fiction Tales 1: 51BC-1638AD

This first anthology, contains the earliest science fiction tales ever written, including:

The Dream of Scipio, True History, Icaro-Menippus, Urashima Taro, The Ebony Horse, The City of Brass, The Tale of the Bamboo Cutter and *The Man in the Moone.*

Early Science Fiction Tales 2: 1648-1844

Stories written before the time of Verne and Wells including:

Micromegas by Voltaire, The Conversation of Eiros

and Charmion by Edgar Allan Poe, The Birthmark by Nathaniel Hawthorne, and other tales.

Our eBooks include:

The Man in the Moone by Francis Godwin – This tale, first published in 1638, tells of a man's journey to the Moon where he discovers a Utopian world.

Micromegas by Voltaire – First published in 1752, this story tells of two giant extraterrestrials who travel across the solar system, eventually reaching the Earth where they meet and enter into a discourse with philosophers. This tale is unusual in that one of the extraterrestrial beings is from a planet orbiting another star. Until this point the aliens of early science fiction had tended to come from within our solar system.

We hope to add more works to our growing collection, and for more information on the latest publications please visit:

www.firestonebooks.com

You can also find out more by following us on Facebook and Twitter